BATMAN™

BATMAN'S WORLD

Written by Nicole Reynolds

Batman created by Bob Kane with Bill Finger

Project Editor Matt Jones
Editorial Assistant Nicole Reynolds
Project Art Editor Stefan Georgiou
Designer Thelma-Jane Robb
Senior Production Editor Jennifer Murray
Senior Production Controller Mary Slater
Managing Editor Sarah Harland
Managing Art Editor Vicky Short
Publishing Director Mark Searle

Reading Consultant: Barbara Marinak

First American Edition, 2021
Published in the United States by DK Publishing
1450 Broadway, Suite 801, New York, NY 10018

Page design copyright © 2021 Dorling Kindersley Limited
DK, a Division of Penguin Random House LLC
21 22 23 24 25 10 9 8 7 6 5 4 3 2 1
001–323479–Sept/2021

A catalog record for this book is available from the Library of Congress.

PB ISBN 978-0-7440-3971-9
HB ISBN 978-0-7440-3972-6

DK books are available at special discounts when purchased in bulk
for sales promotions, premiums, fund-raising, or educational use.
For details, contact: DK Publishing Special Markets,
1450 Broadway, Suite 801, New York, NY 10018
SpecialSales@dk.com

Printed and bound in China

For the curious

www.dk.com

Contents

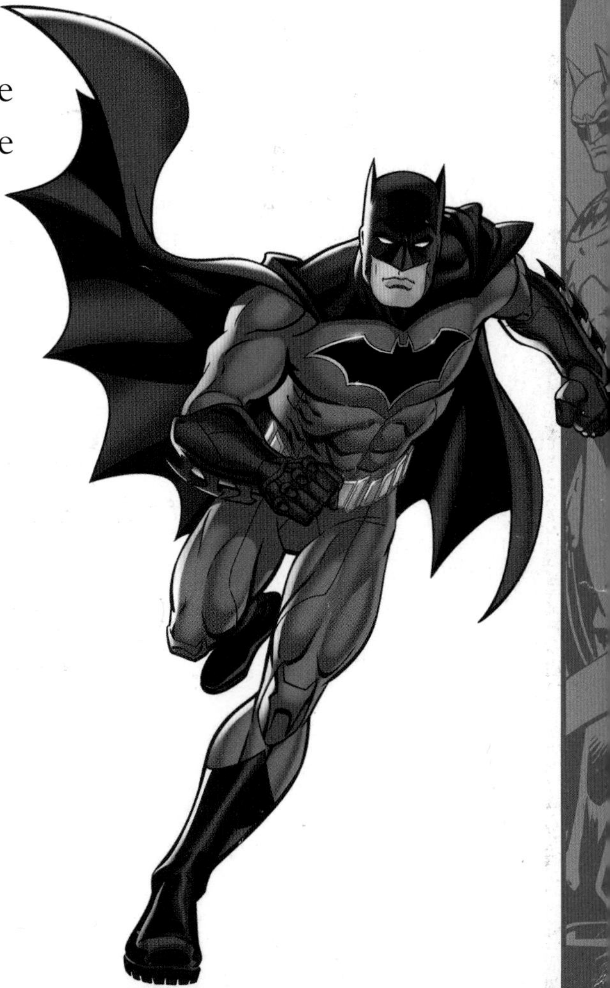

Meet Batman

Meet Batman! He is a Super Hero who protects Gotham City from criminals. Batman is also known as The Dark Knight because he is brave and honorable. He uses his intelligence, fighting skills, and gadgets to defeat Super-Villains.

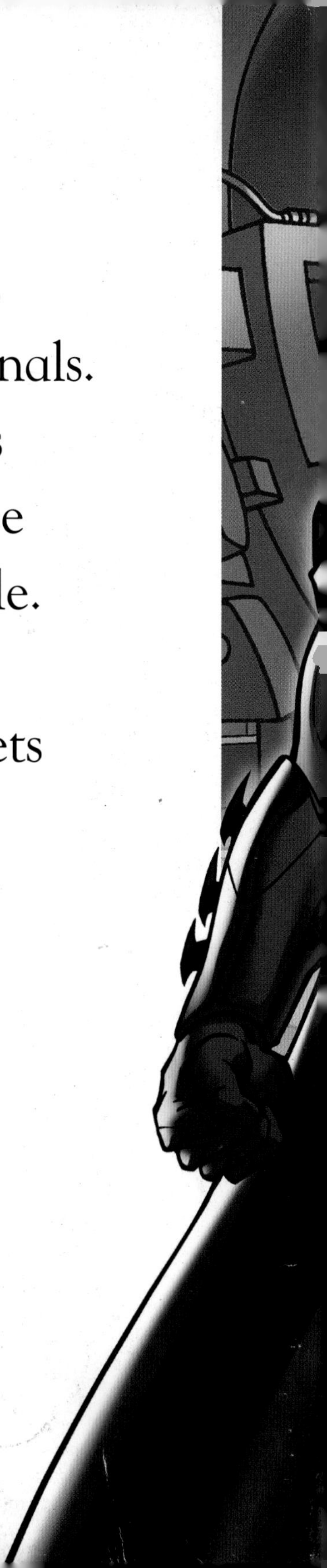

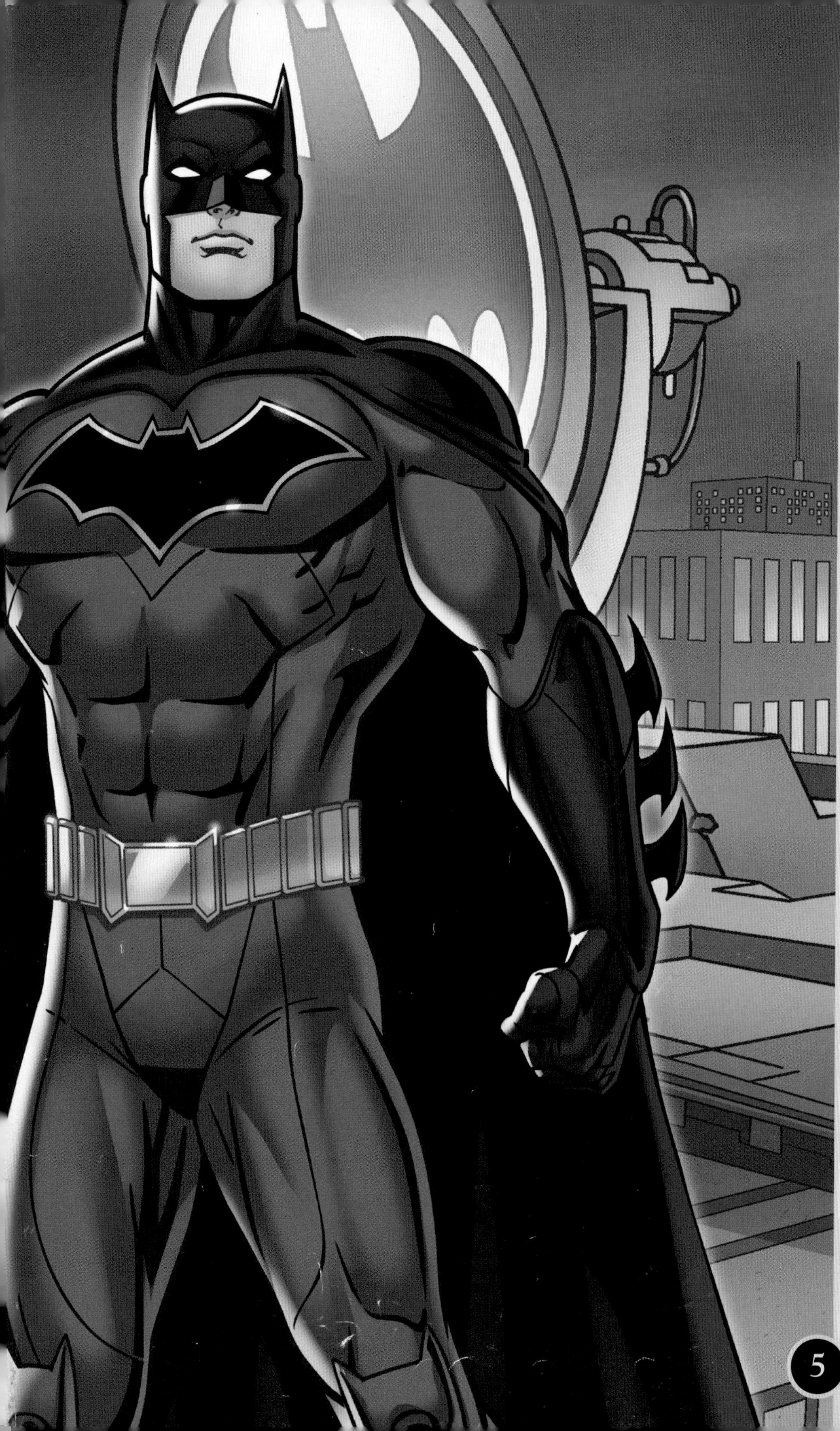

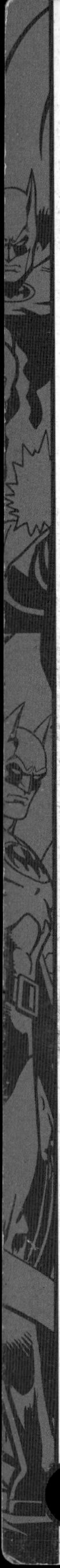

Gotham City

Gotham City is a huge city with lots of problems. There are many dangerous criminals causing trouble and committing crimes. Commissioner Gordon is in charge of the police in Gotham City. He needs Batman's help to keep people safe.

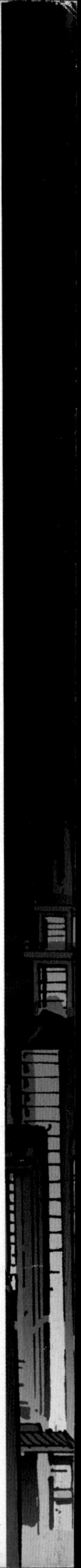

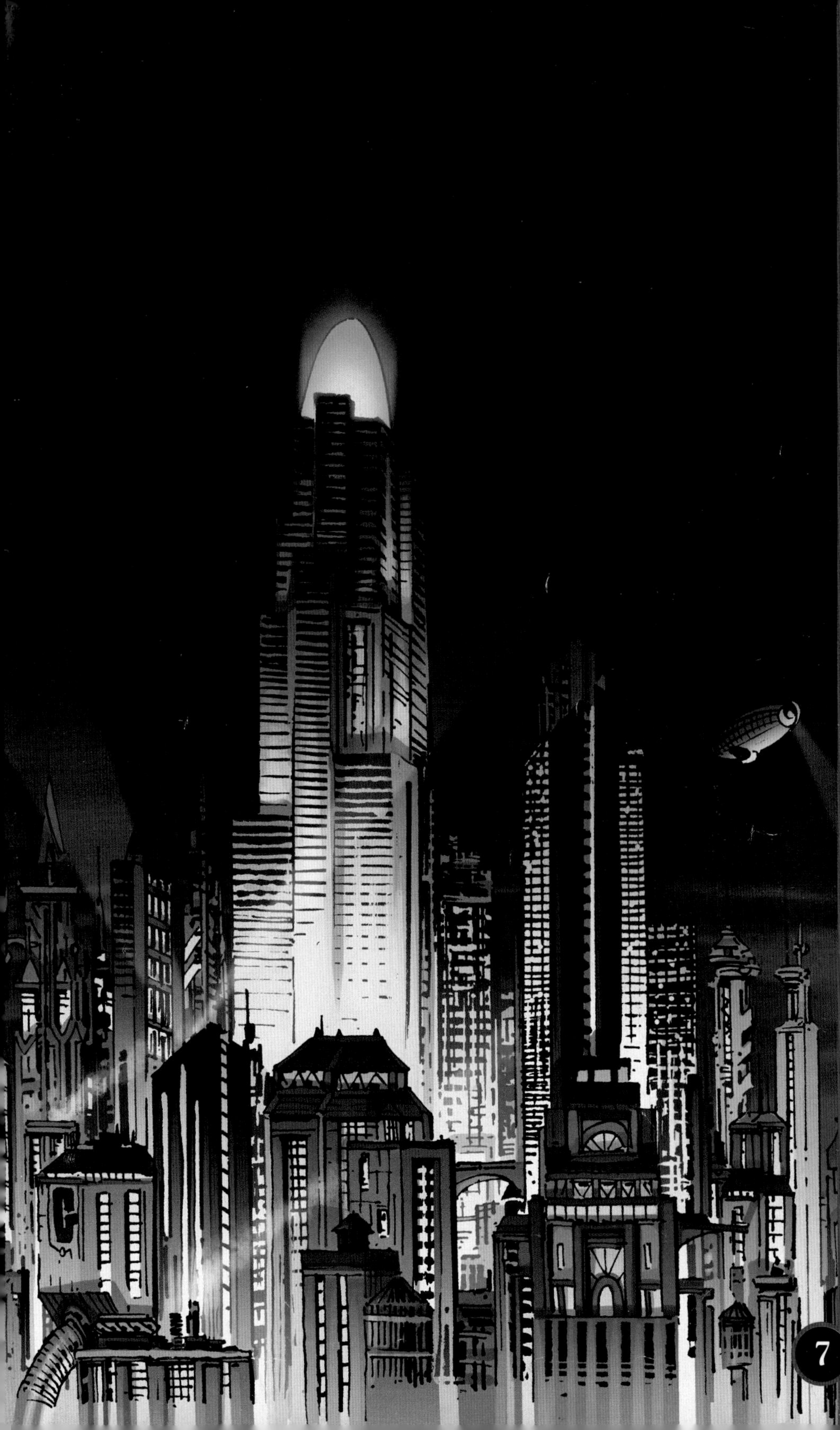

What is Batman's secret identity?

Batman's real name is Bruce Wayne. He is the rich and famous CEO of Wayne Industries. The company creates many exciting things, such as new technology.

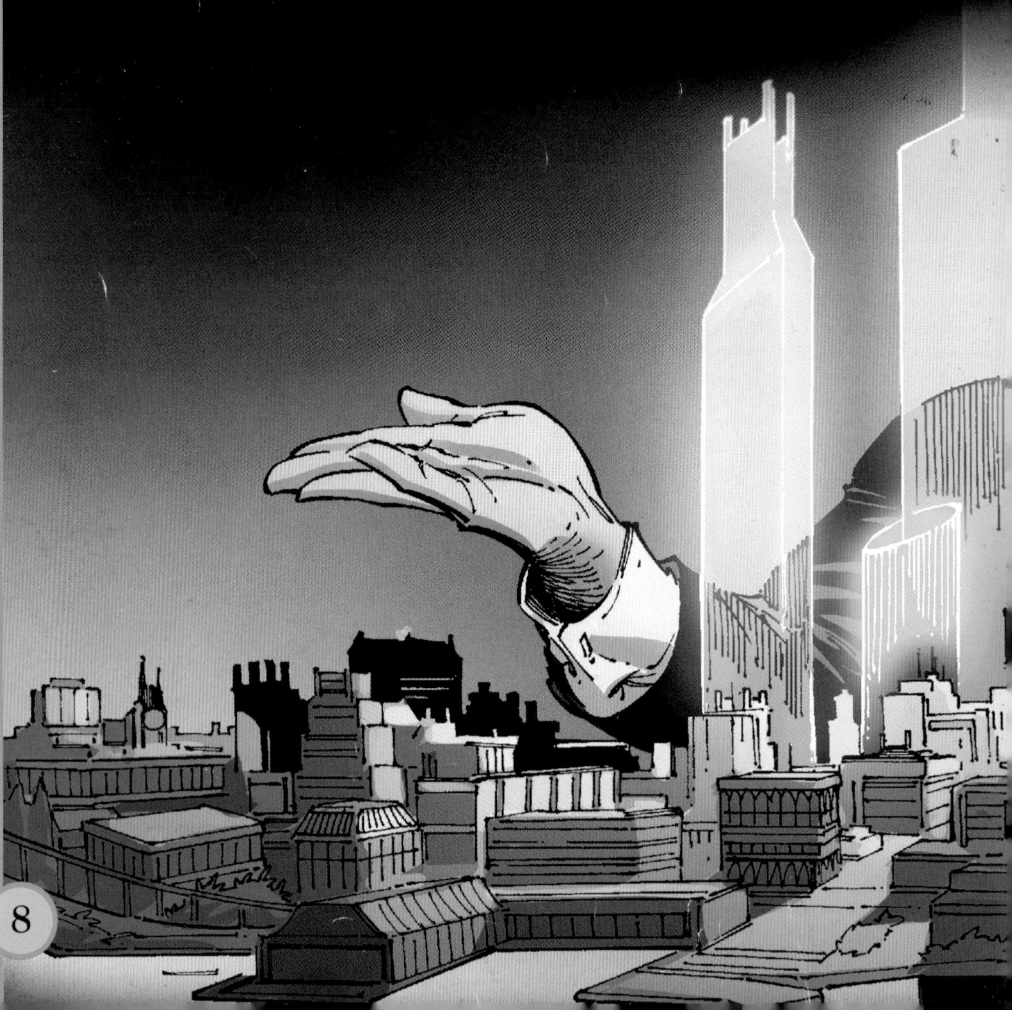

Bruce spends lots of time being Batman. His friend Lucius Fox helps run Wayne Industries.

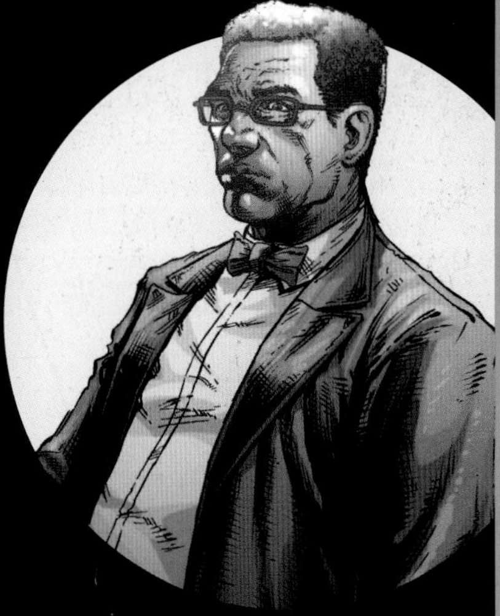

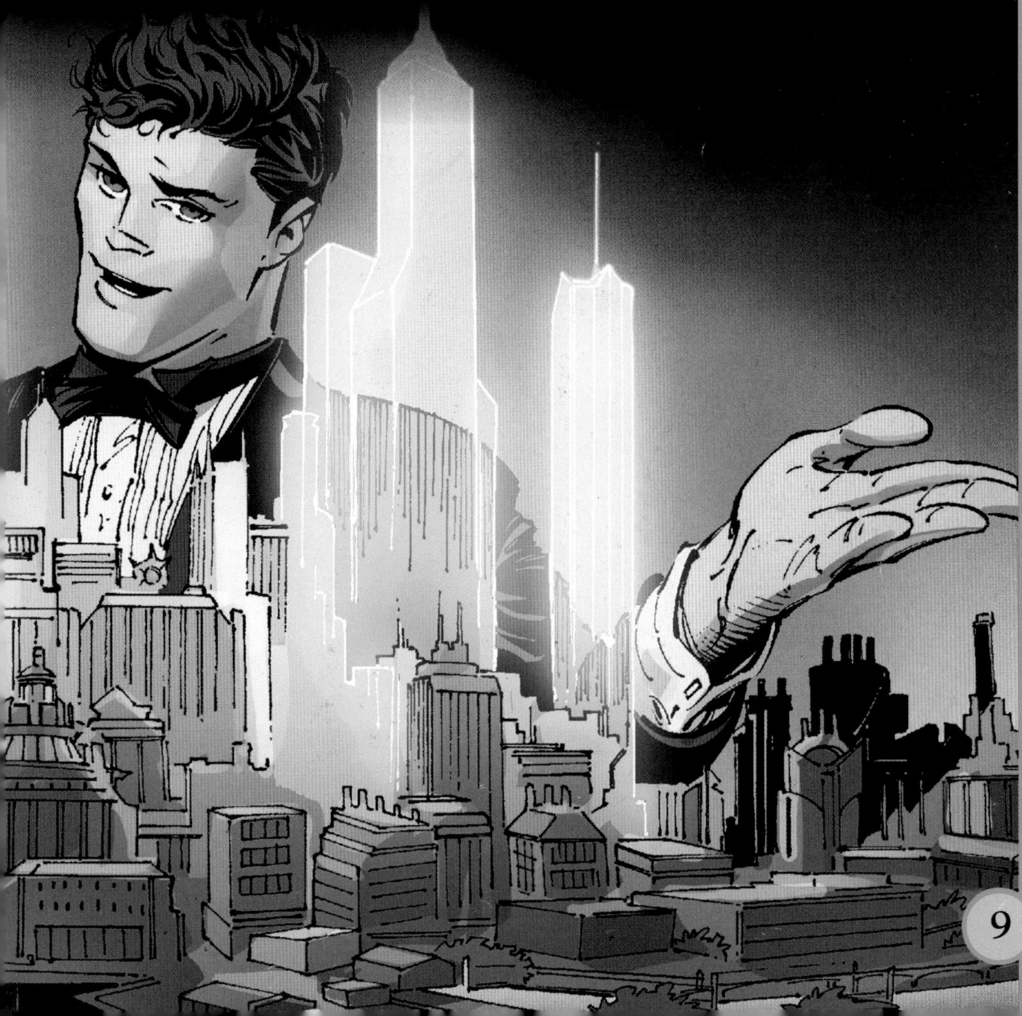

Wayne Manor

Wayne Manor is Bruce Wayne's family home. It is very grand. Bruce lives there with his butler, Alfred Pennyworth.

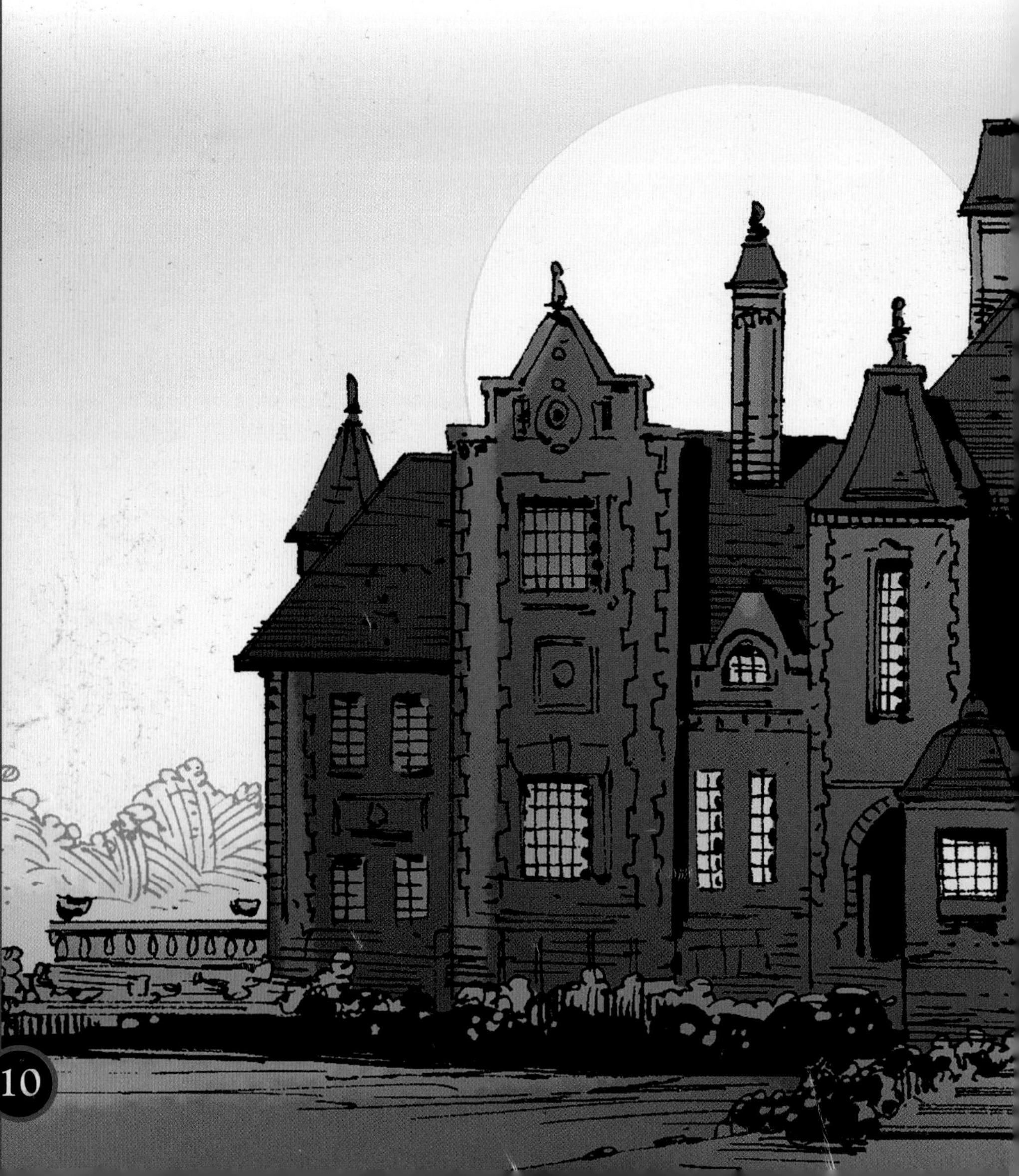

Wayne Manor has
a secret. There is
a hidden base
named the Batcave
under the house!

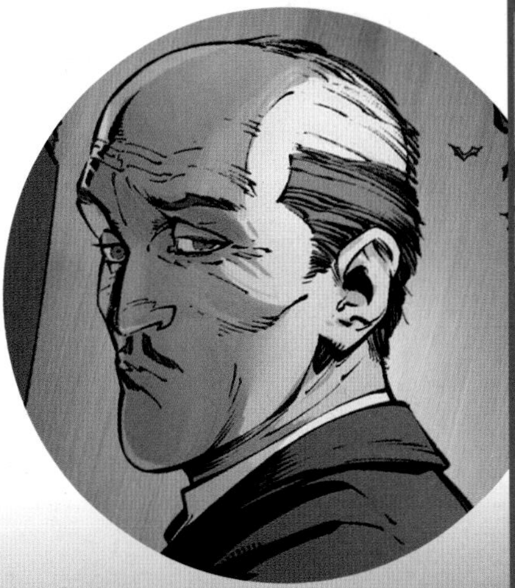

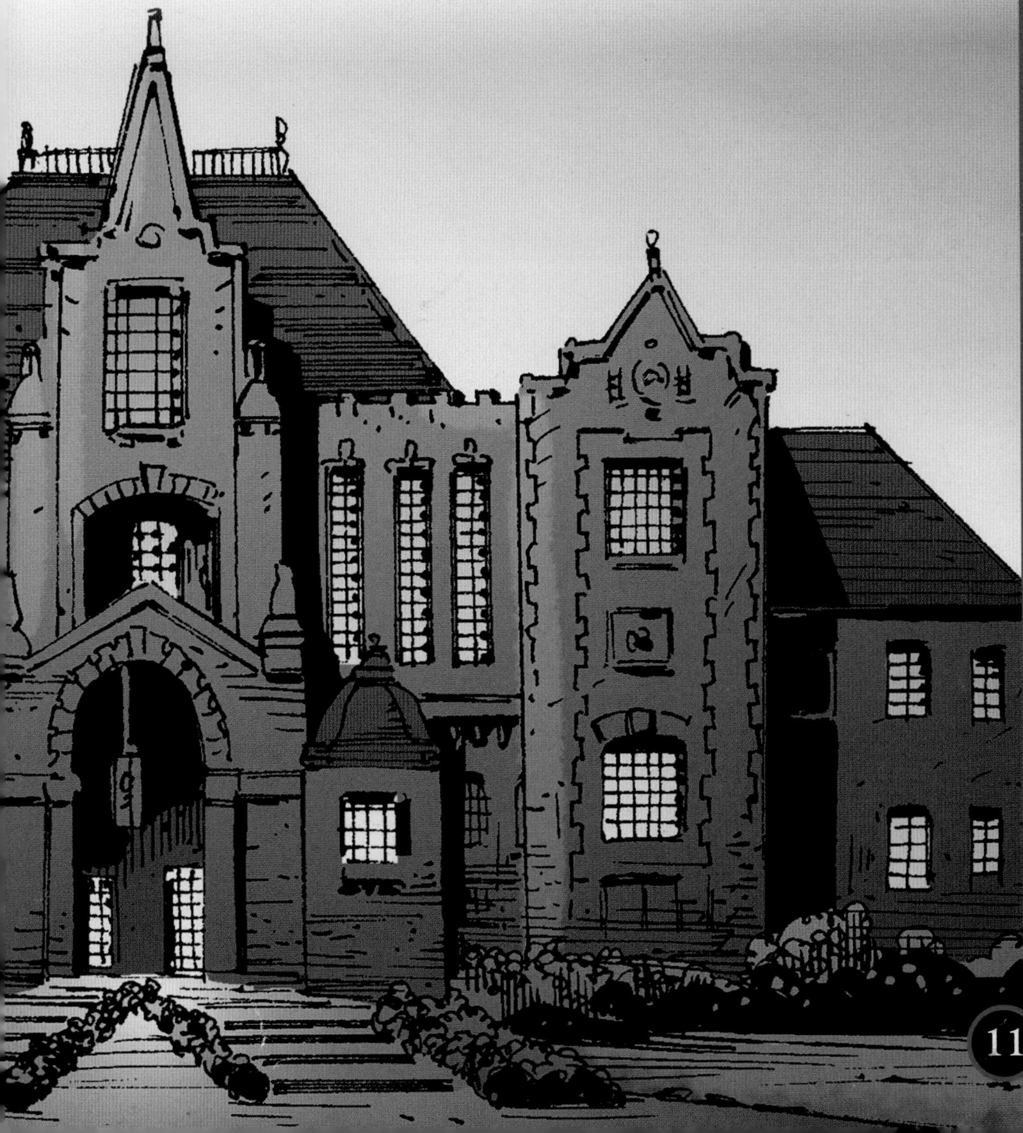

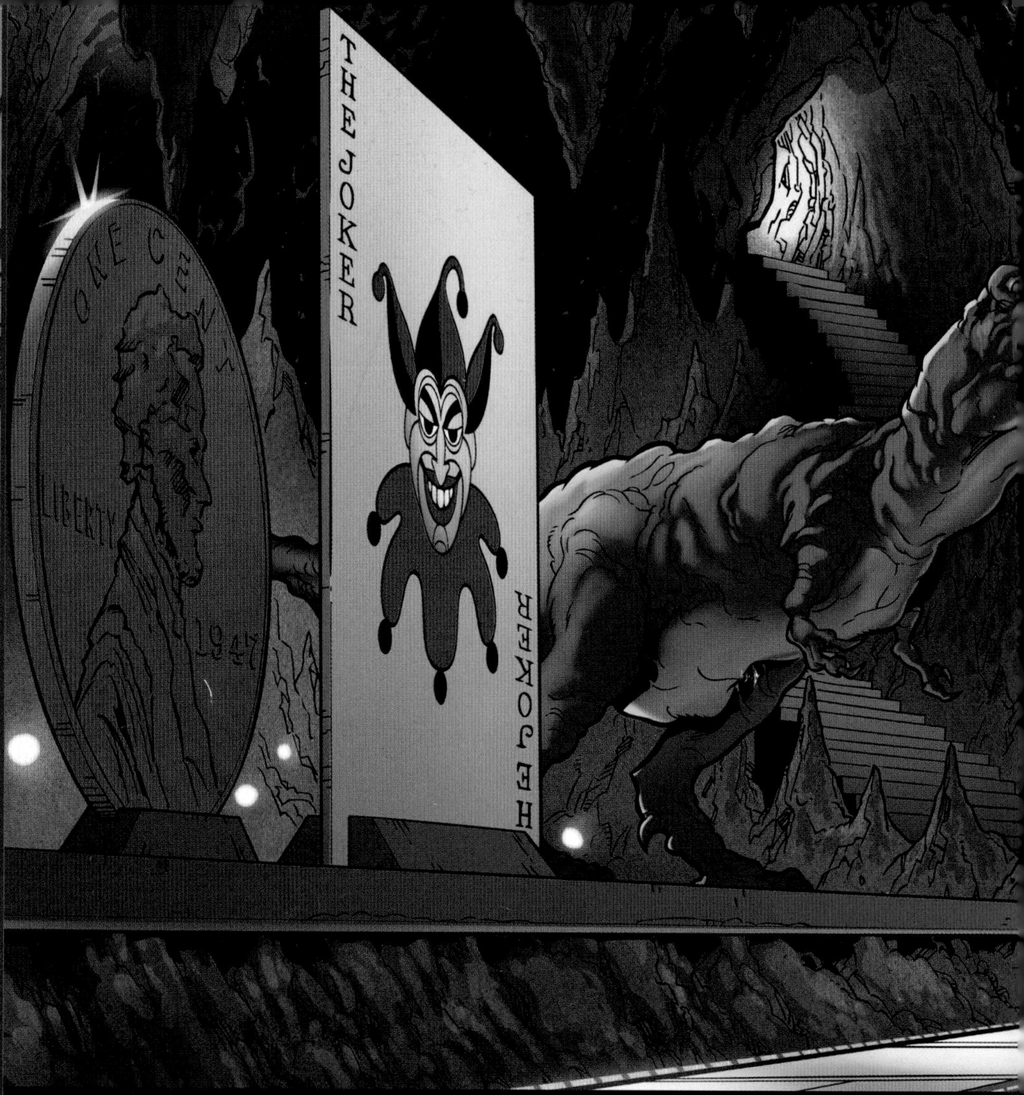
THE JOKER
LIBERTY
1947

The Batcave

Quick, to the Batcave! The Batcave has lots of cool technology to help Batman fight crime. The most important gadget is the Batcomputer. It monitors crime around the world.

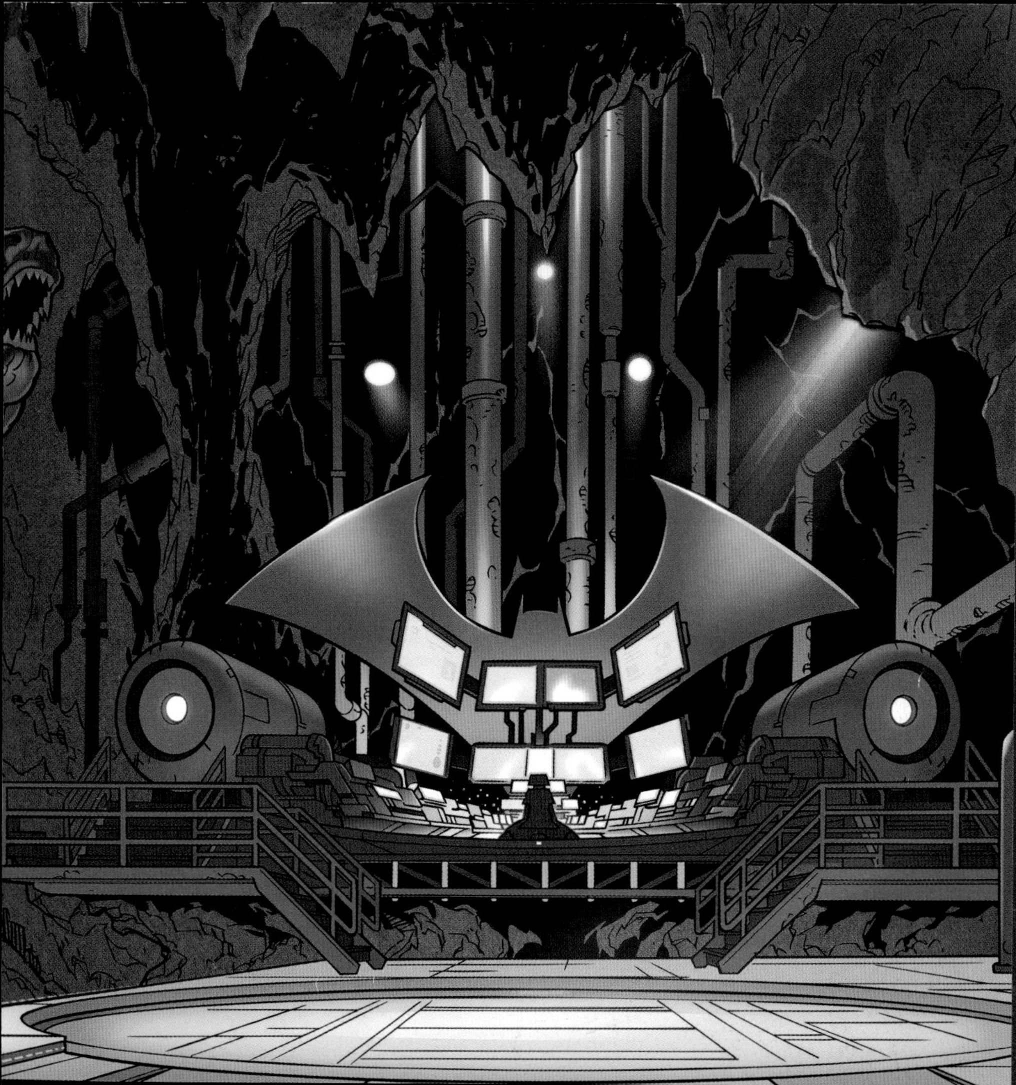

Batman also uses the Batcave to store objects he has collected on his adventures. He even has a robot dinosaur!

Unique vehicles

These vehicles allow Batman to fight crime anywhere! He can travel quickly over land, sea, and air.

The **Batplane** can fly to any part of the world.

The **Bat-glider** is perfect for quiet journeys.

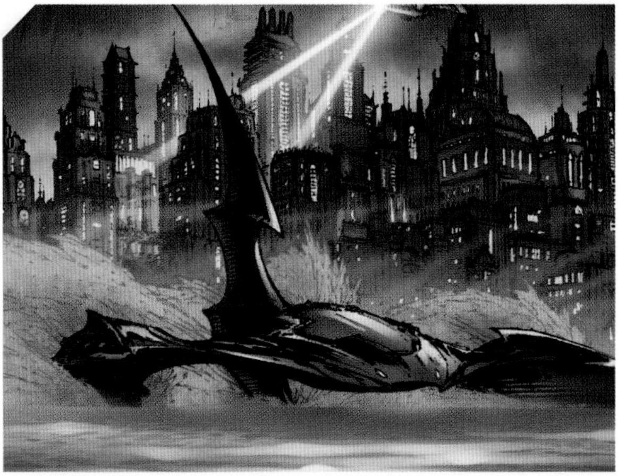

The **Batboat** has a submarine and a jet ski.

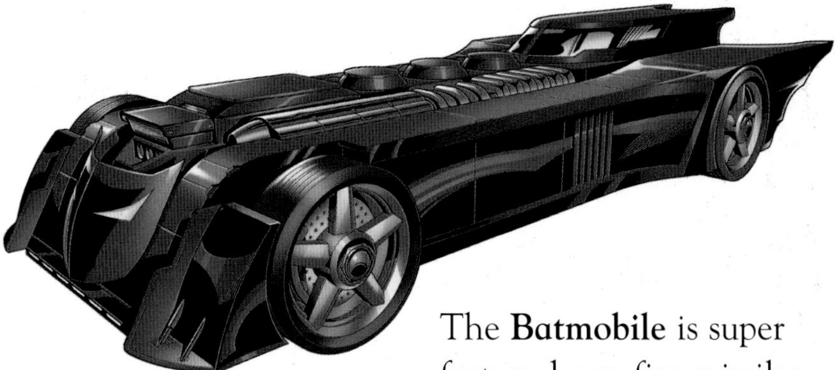

The **Batmobile** is super fast and can fire missiles.

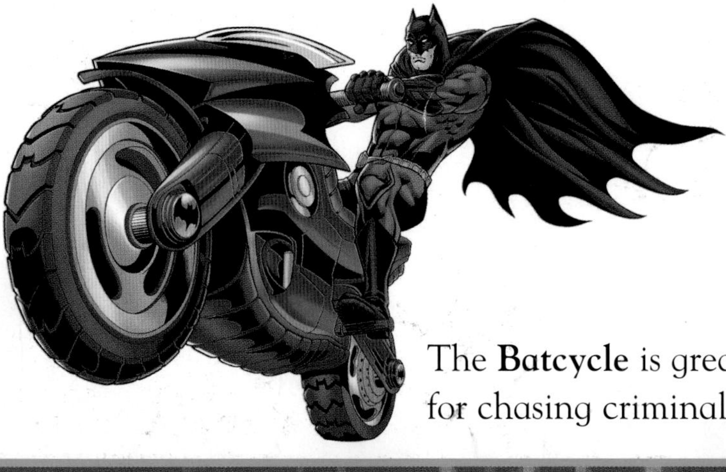

The **Batcycle** is great for chasing criminals.

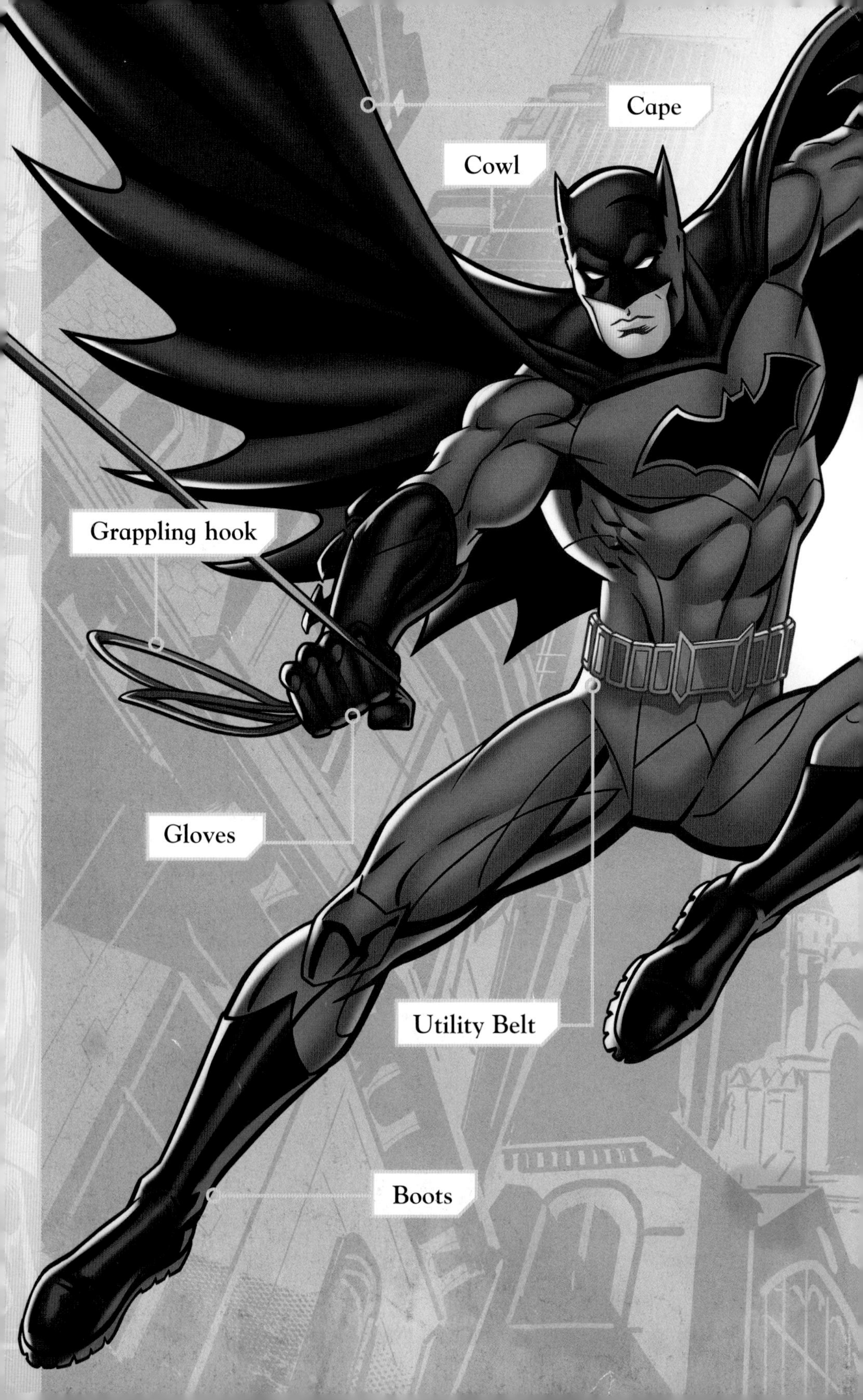
Cape
Cowl
Grappling hook
Gloves
Utility Belt
Boots

Batman's Batsuit

Batman wears a special suit called the Batsuit. The suit protects Batman from getting hurt. The cowl hides his secret identity. Batman's Utility Belt is full of useful gadgets, like a grappling hook. The hook is connected to a rope. Batman uses his grappling hook to climb up Gotham City's tall buildings.

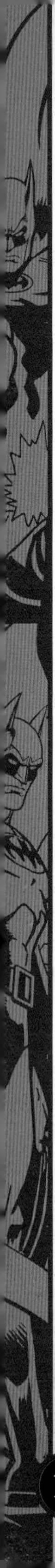

Robin

Batman does not always fight crime alone. He often has help from his friend and sidekick Robin. Robin is very agile and an excellent fighter. Batman and Robin are called the Dynamic Duo. They work together to protect the people of Gotham City.

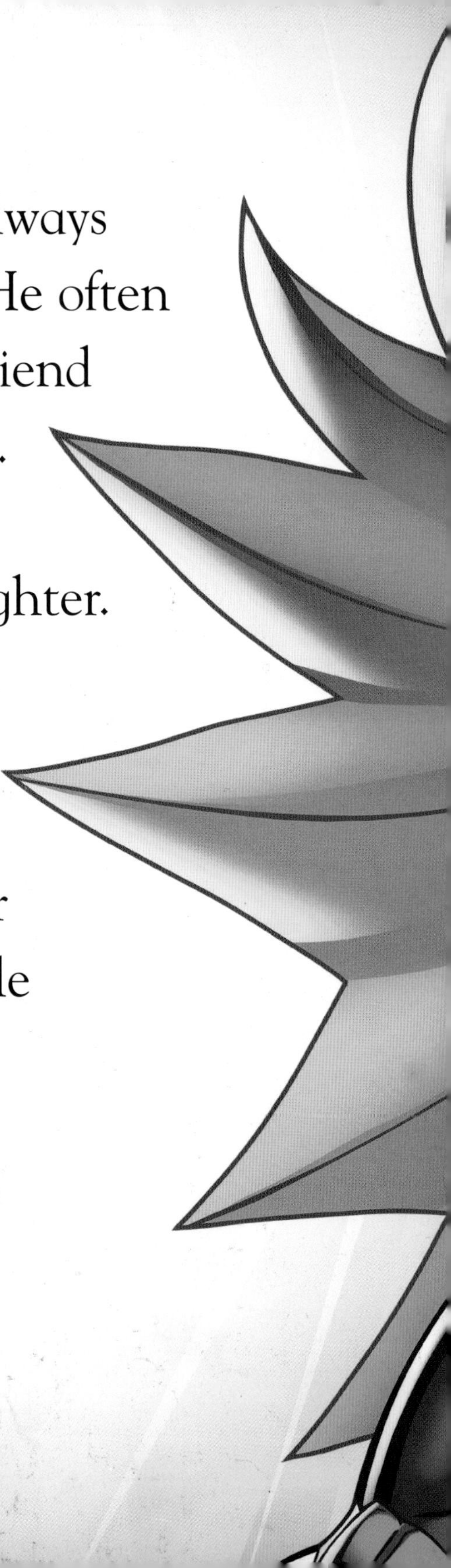

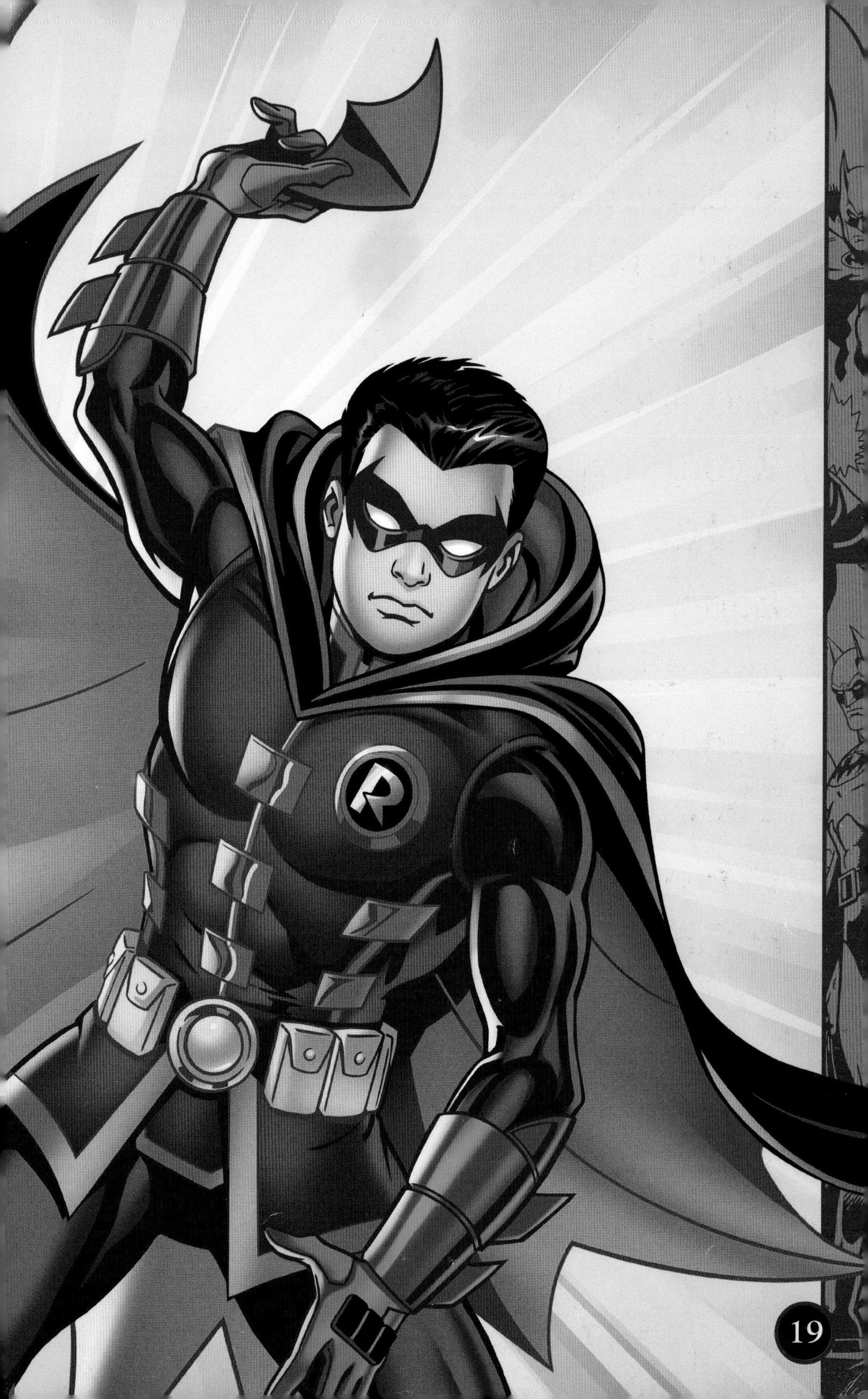

The Bat-Family

Batman also relies on the Bat-Family to help keep Gotham City safe. The Bat-Family is a group of Super Heroes who work with Batman. All of the Super Heroes wear capes and suits, just like Batman.

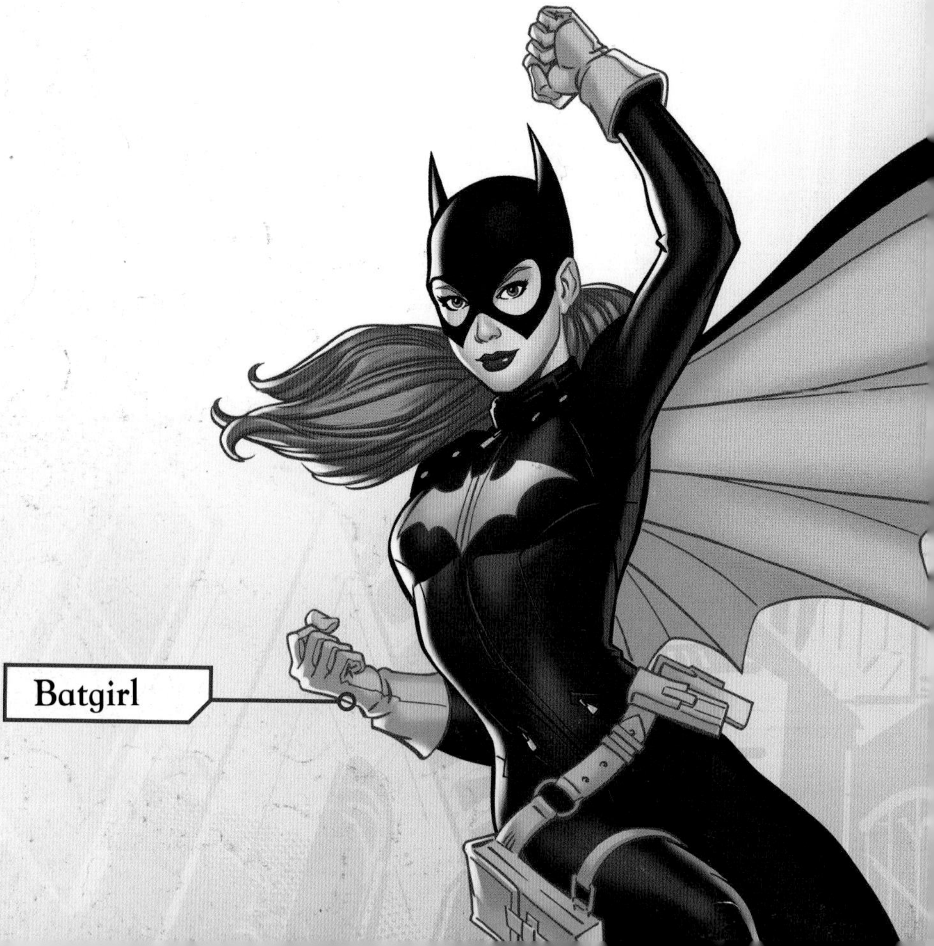
Batgirl

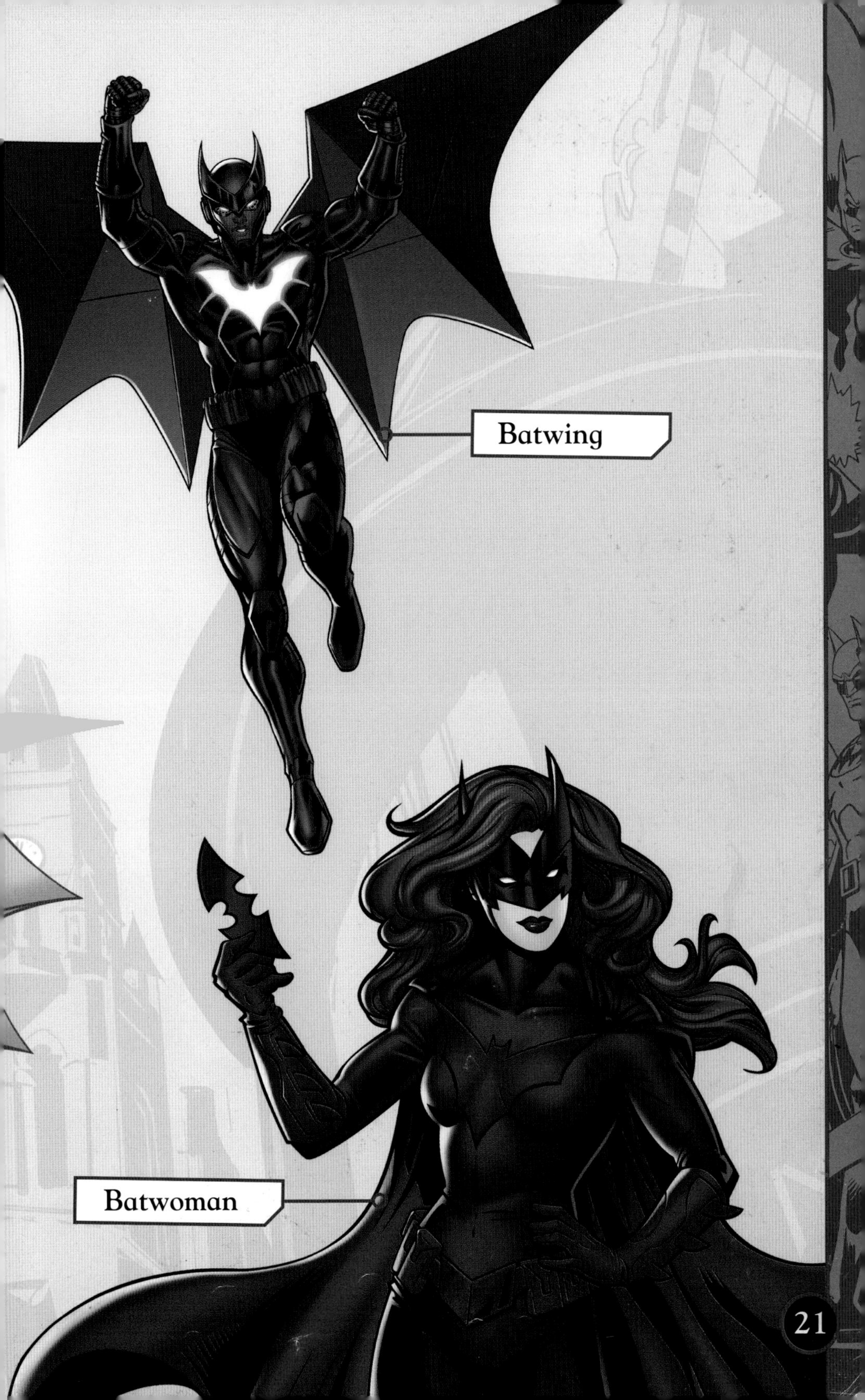
Batwing
Batwoman

Catwoman

Some days Catwoman is a criminal, and other days a hero! She is a talented burglar who steals jewels. But she also helps Batman protect Gotham City.

Like a cat, Catwoman can climb walls and hide in small spaces. She even has sharp claws on her gloves.

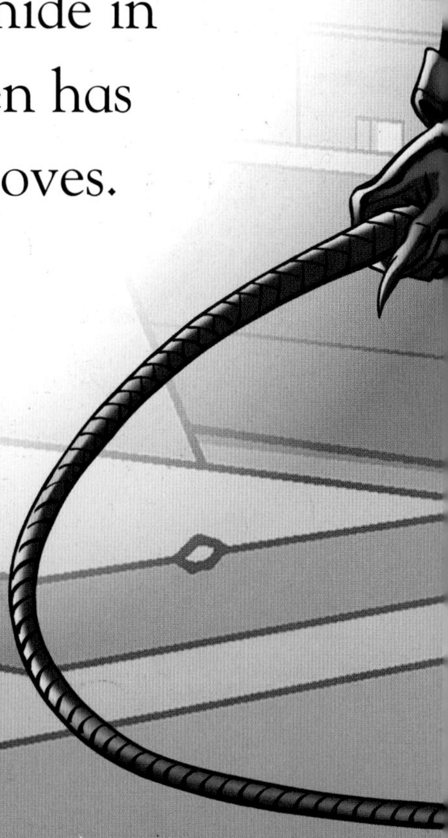

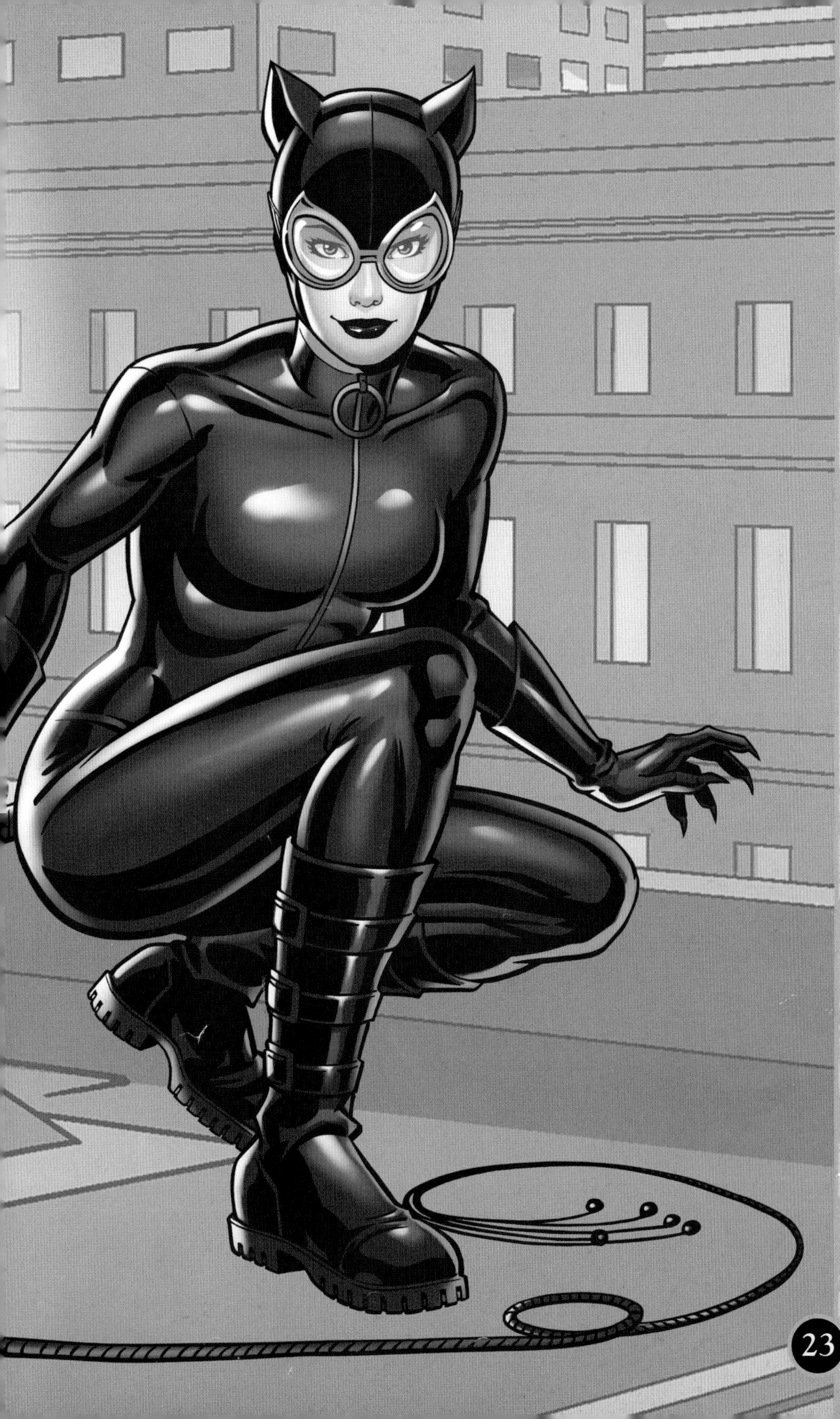

Call to action

There are many
dangerous
Super-Villains in
Gotham City.
The police and
Commissioner
Gordon need
Batman's help
to stop them!

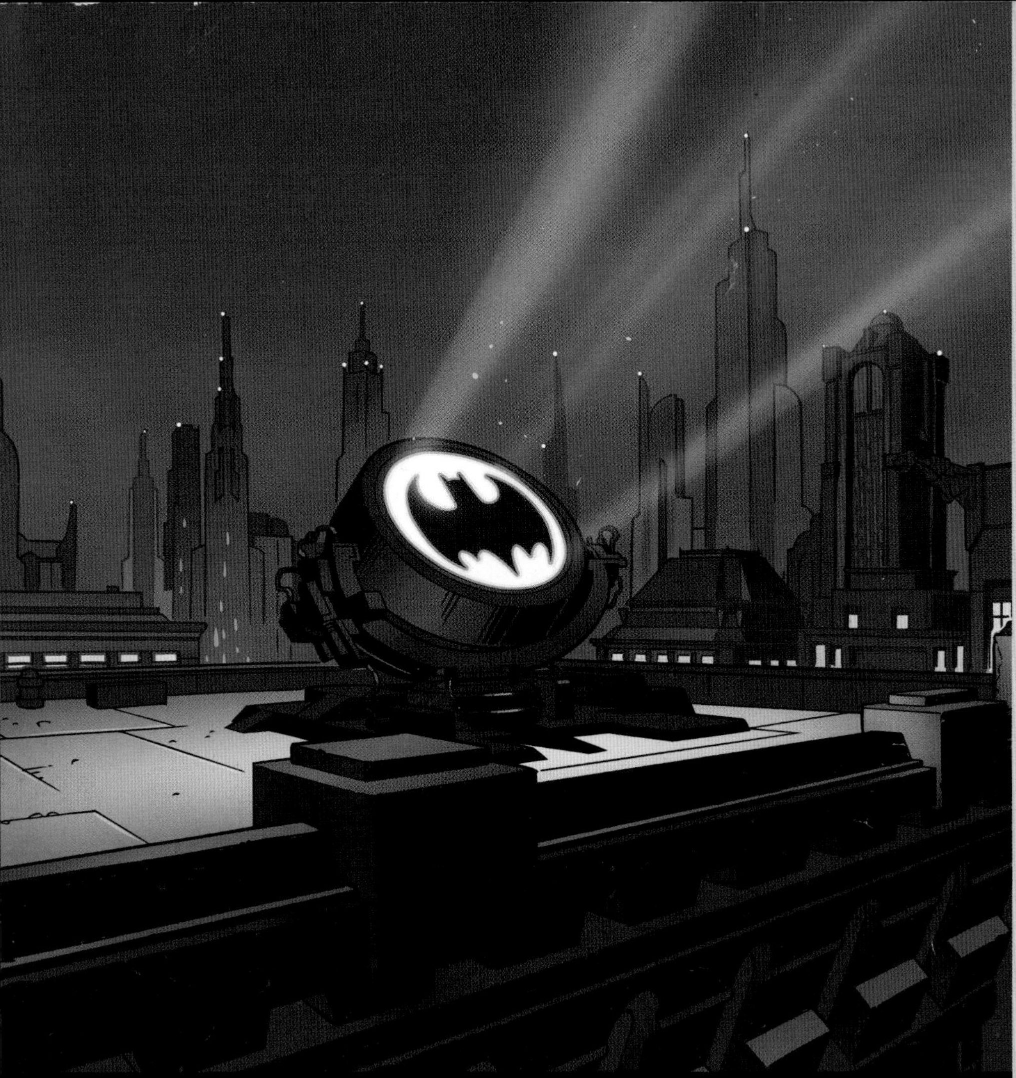

There is a powerful light named the Bat-Signal on top of the police station. When the police need Batman's help, they turn on the light. Then, Batman rushes to help.

The Justice League

The Justice League is a team of powerful Super Heroes. Together they can defeat any threat to Earth! Each member of the group has their own strengths and skills. Sometimes members of the group might disagree, but they know they are stronger together.

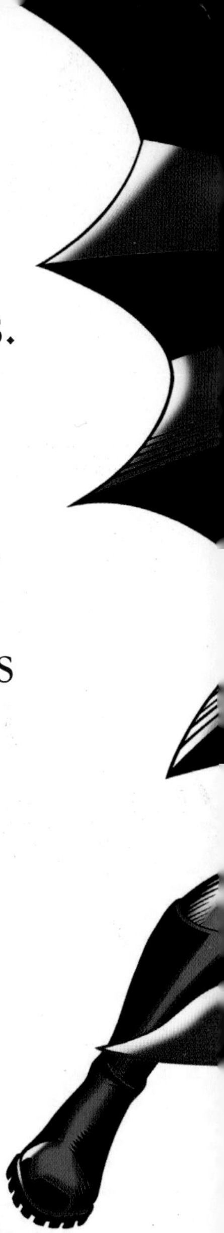

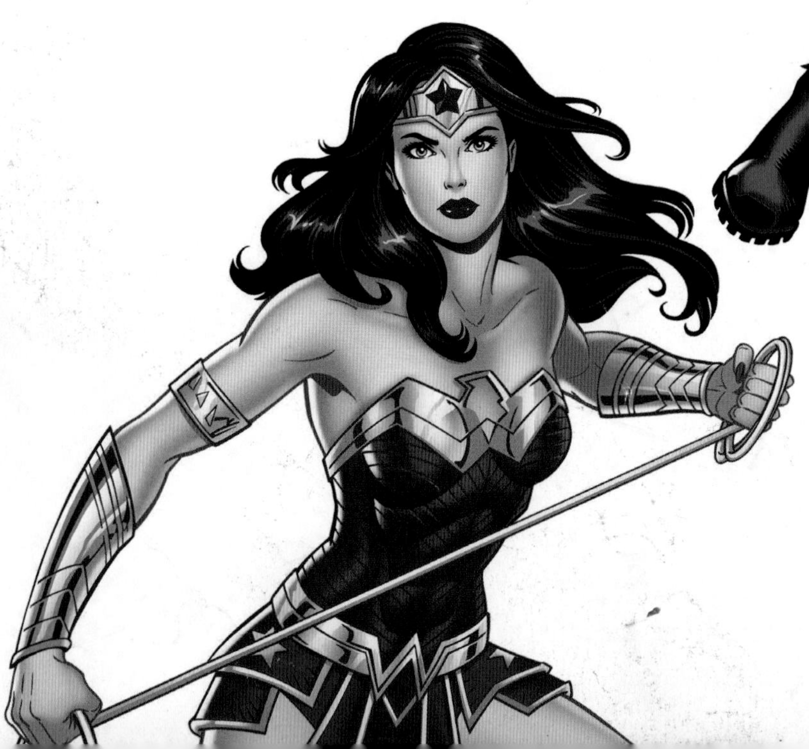

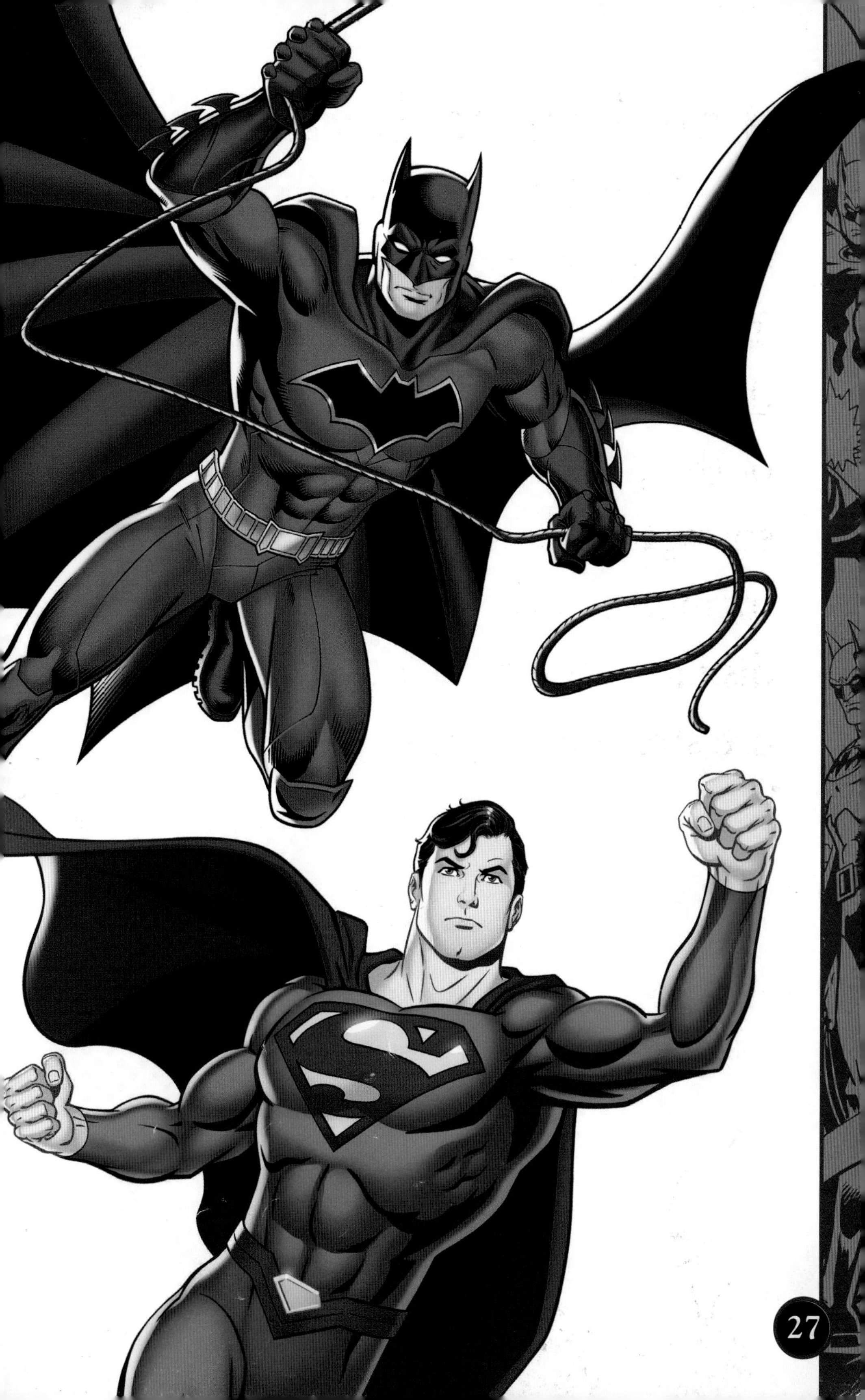

Super Heroes unite

These Super Heroes make a great team. They are all ready to help when the world is in danger!

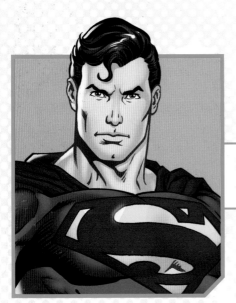

Superman is from the planet Krypton.

Wonder Woman is very strong and wise.

The Flash can move faster than the speed of light.

Aquaman is the King of Atlantis.

Cyborg has many robotic body parts.

Green Lantern is a member of the space police force.

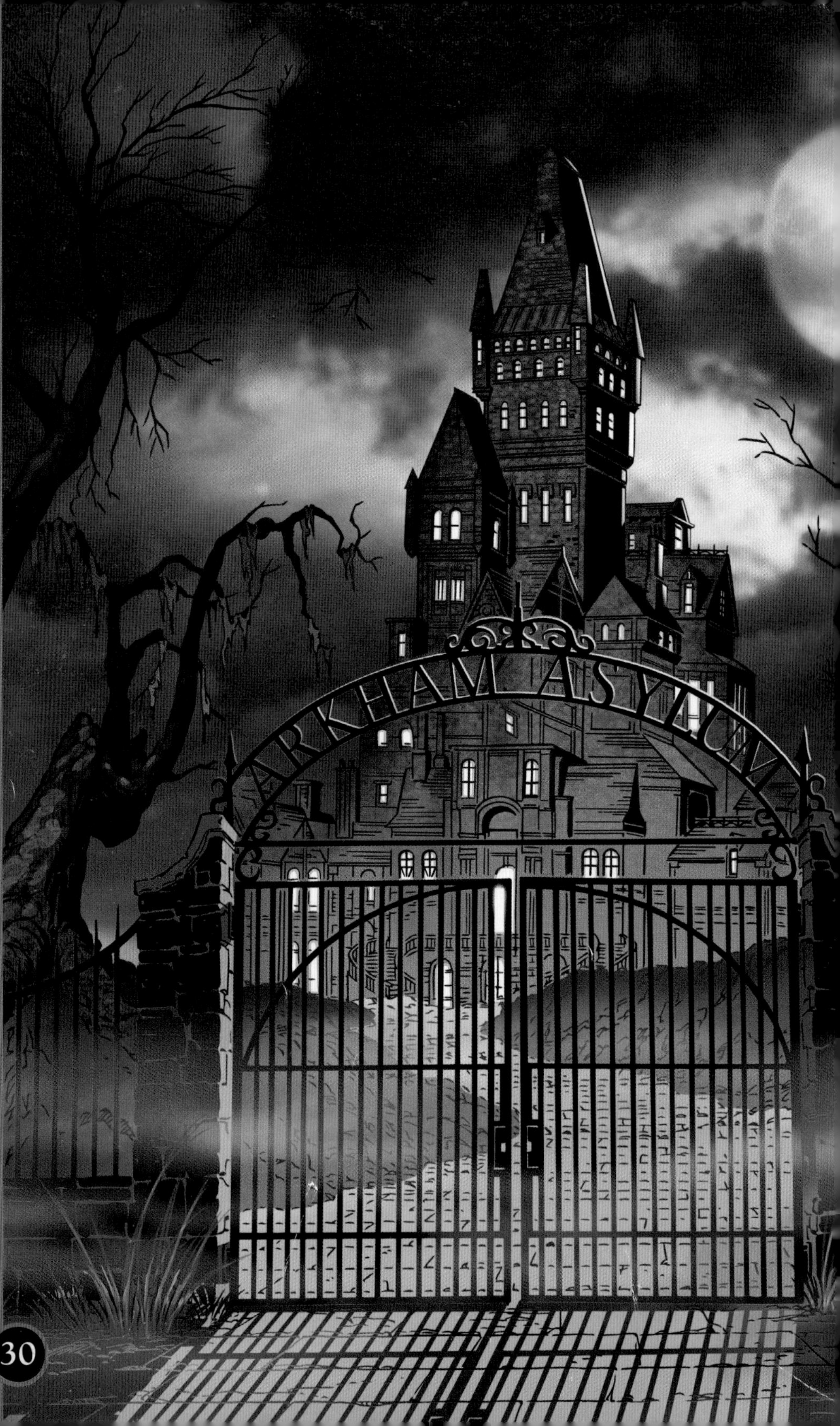
ARKHAM ASYLUM

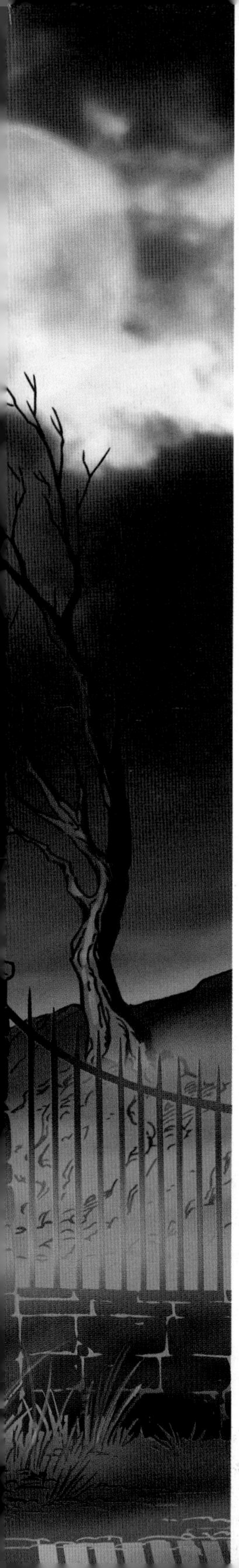

Locked up

Arkham Asylum is a gloomy prison on the edge of Gotham City. When Batman catches dangerous Super-Villains, they are sent there. The Joker has been sent to Arkham Asylum many times. He and other criminals are always trying to escape!

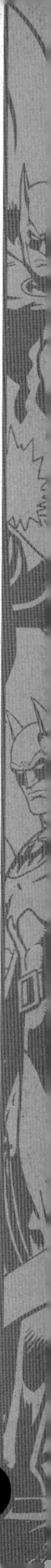

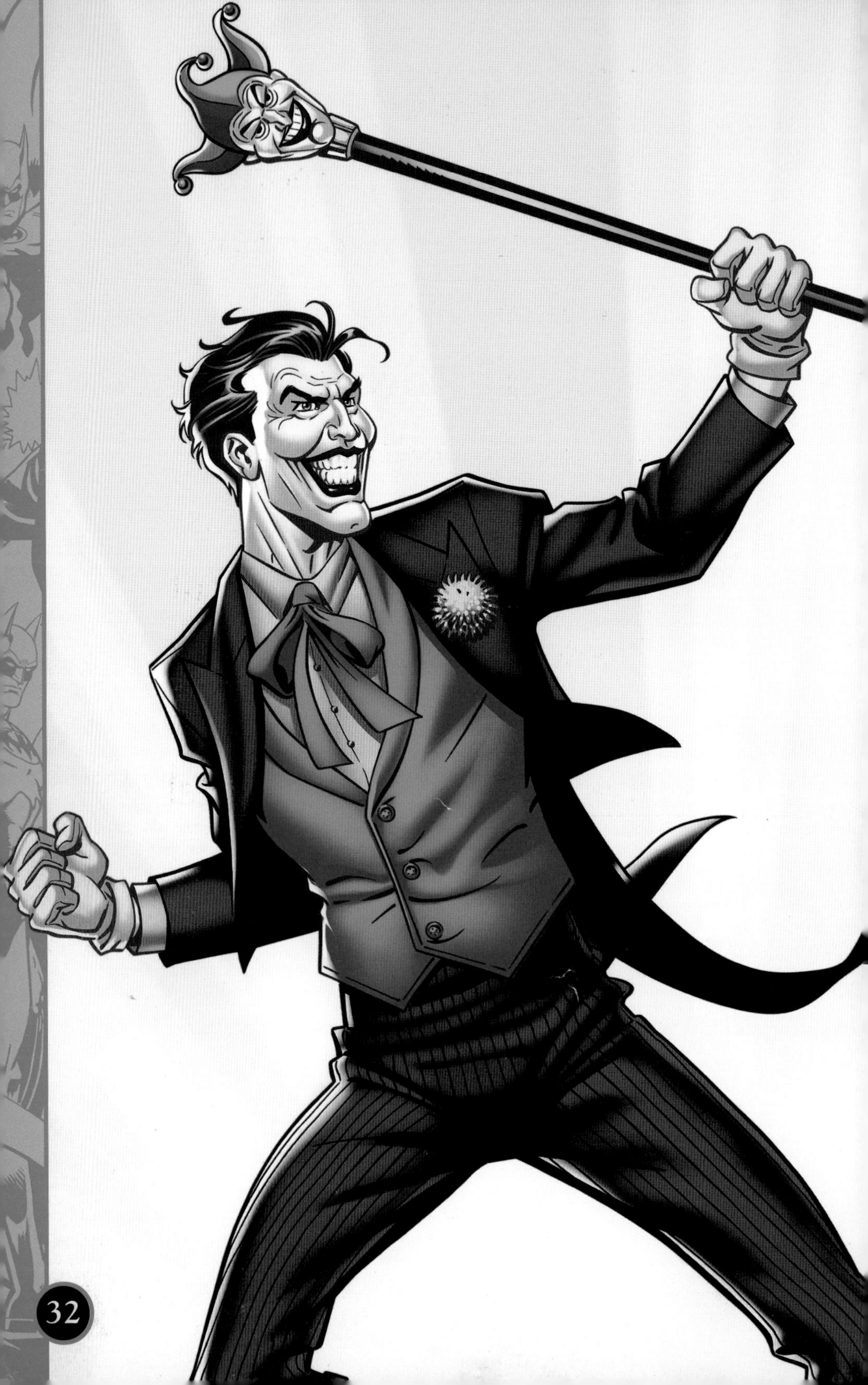

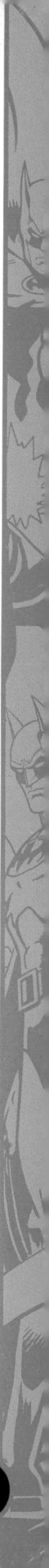

The Joker

The Joker is Batman's worst enemy. They have fought many times.

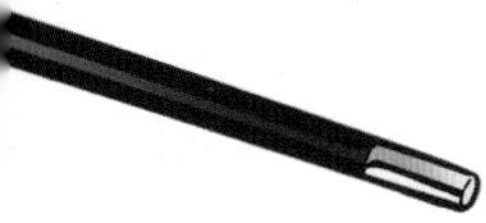

The Joker loves to cause chaos in Gotham City. He uses wacky weapons and vehicles to carry out his schemes. Everything is a joke to The Joker, even committing crimes!

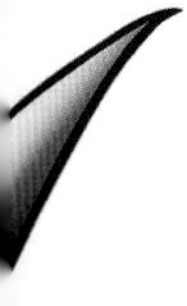

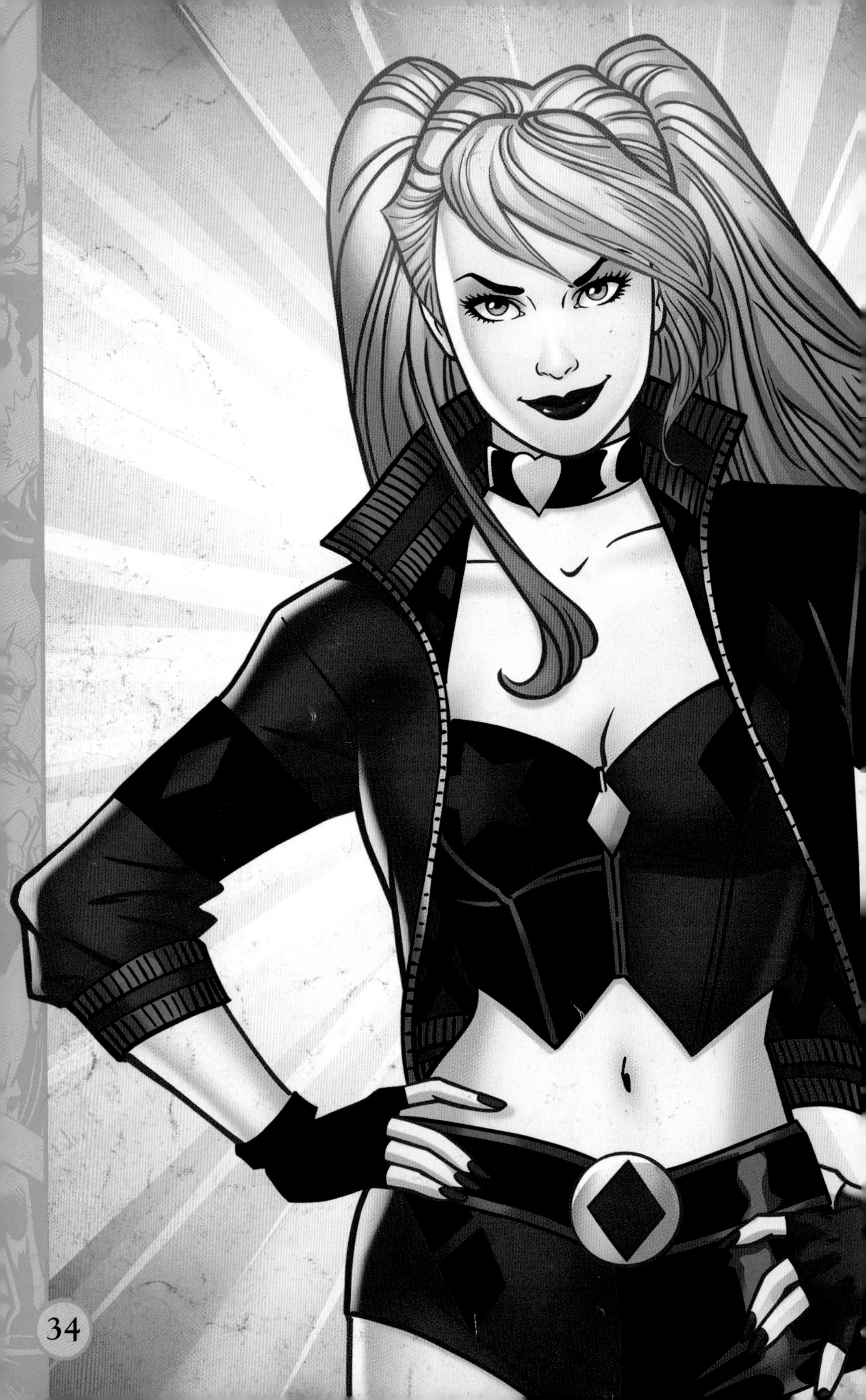

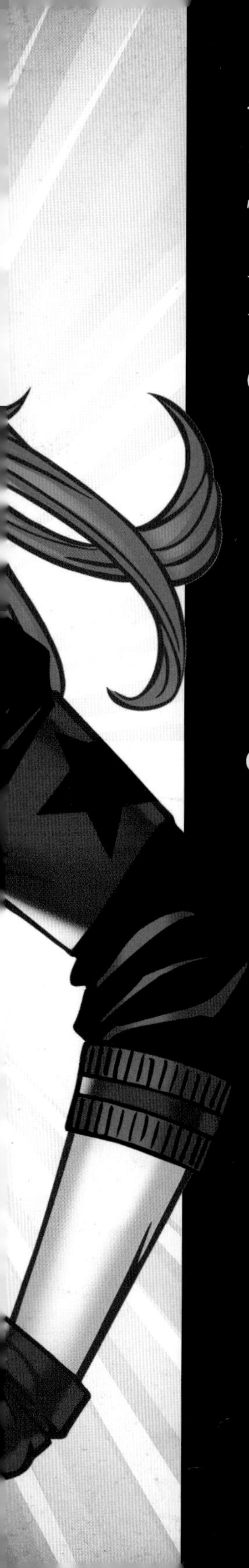

Harley Quinn

The colorful criminal Harley Quinn was once a doctor at Arkham Asylum. She now enjoys making trouble. Harley likes to work in a team. She will sometimes team up with other Super-Villains, or even Super Heroes. Harley Quinn does whatever she wants!

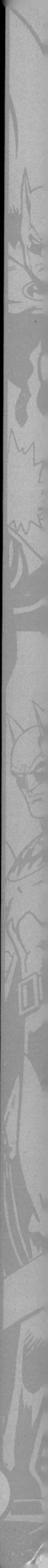

Chasing crime

Batman is always ready for any situation. Sometimes he has to chase and fight Super-Villains. Batman is very strong and has fought many tough battles. He uses his strength and quick thinking to catch the criminals every time!

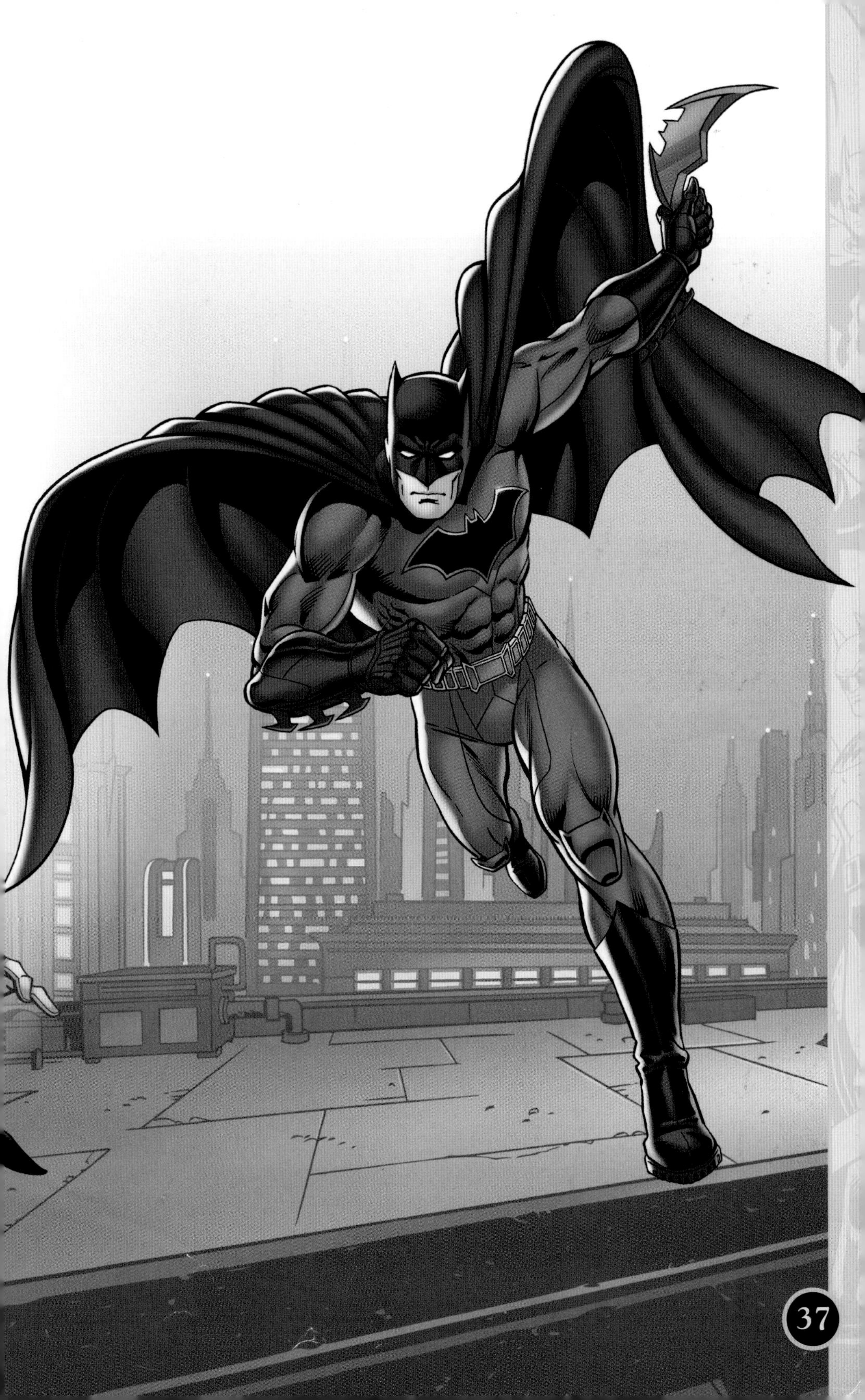

The Riddler

Can you guess which villain this is? It's the Riddler! This confusing criminal loves puzzles and riddles. He even has a question mark on his cane. The Riddler leaves clues at crime scenes for Batman. They can be very difficult to solve!

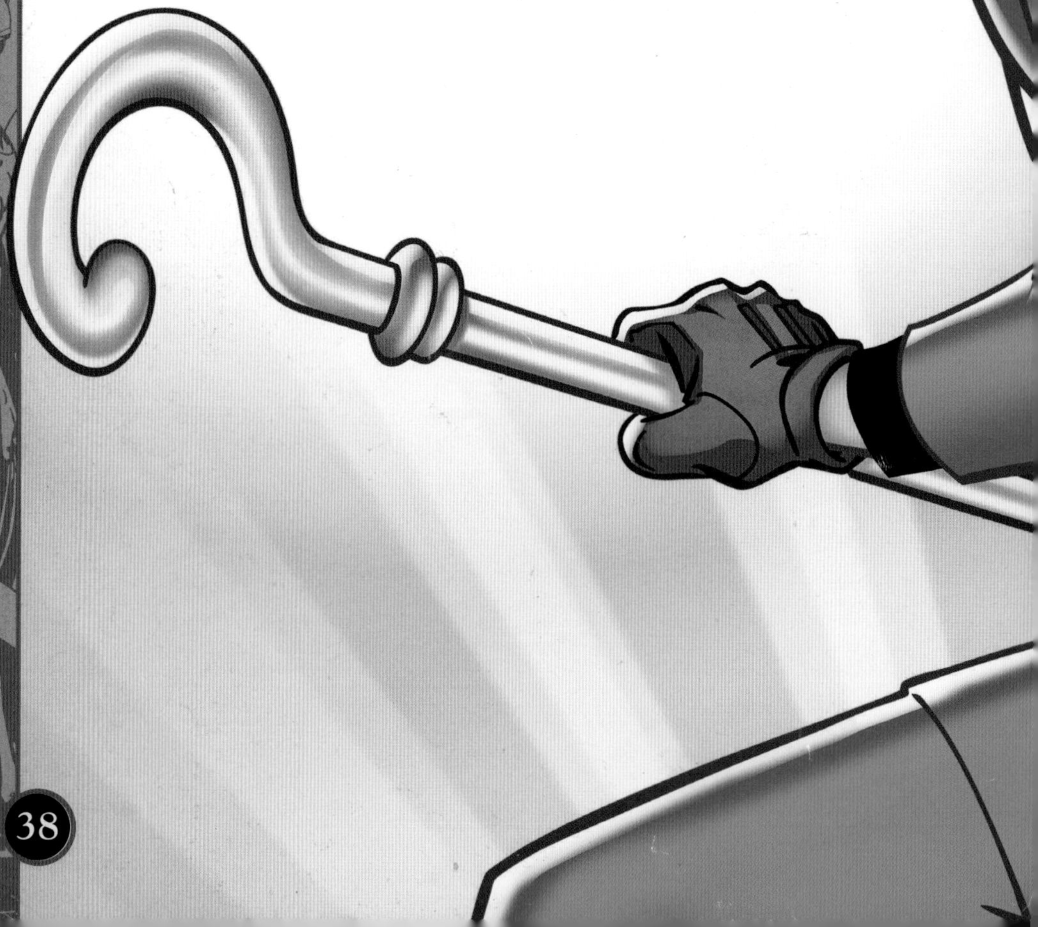

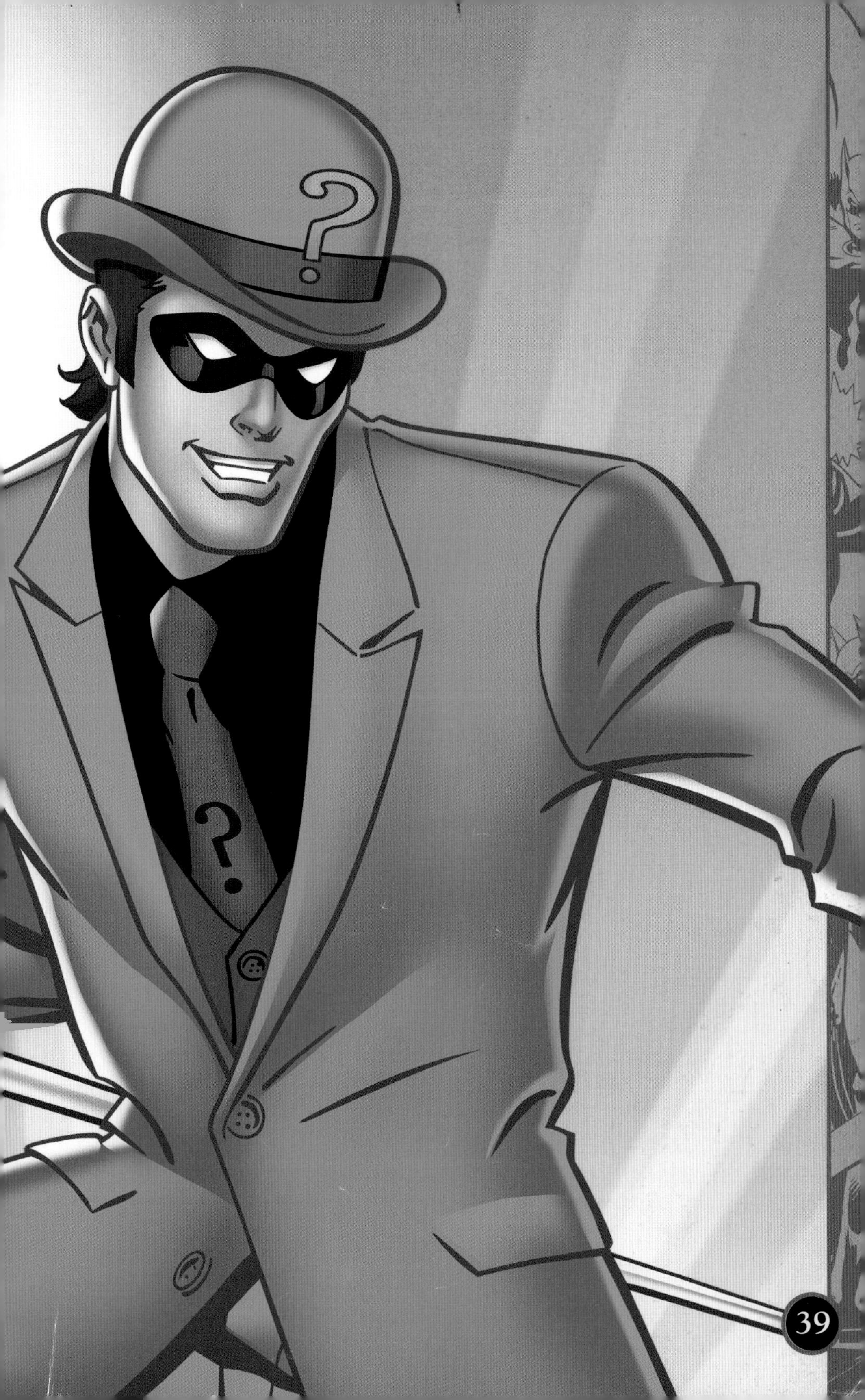

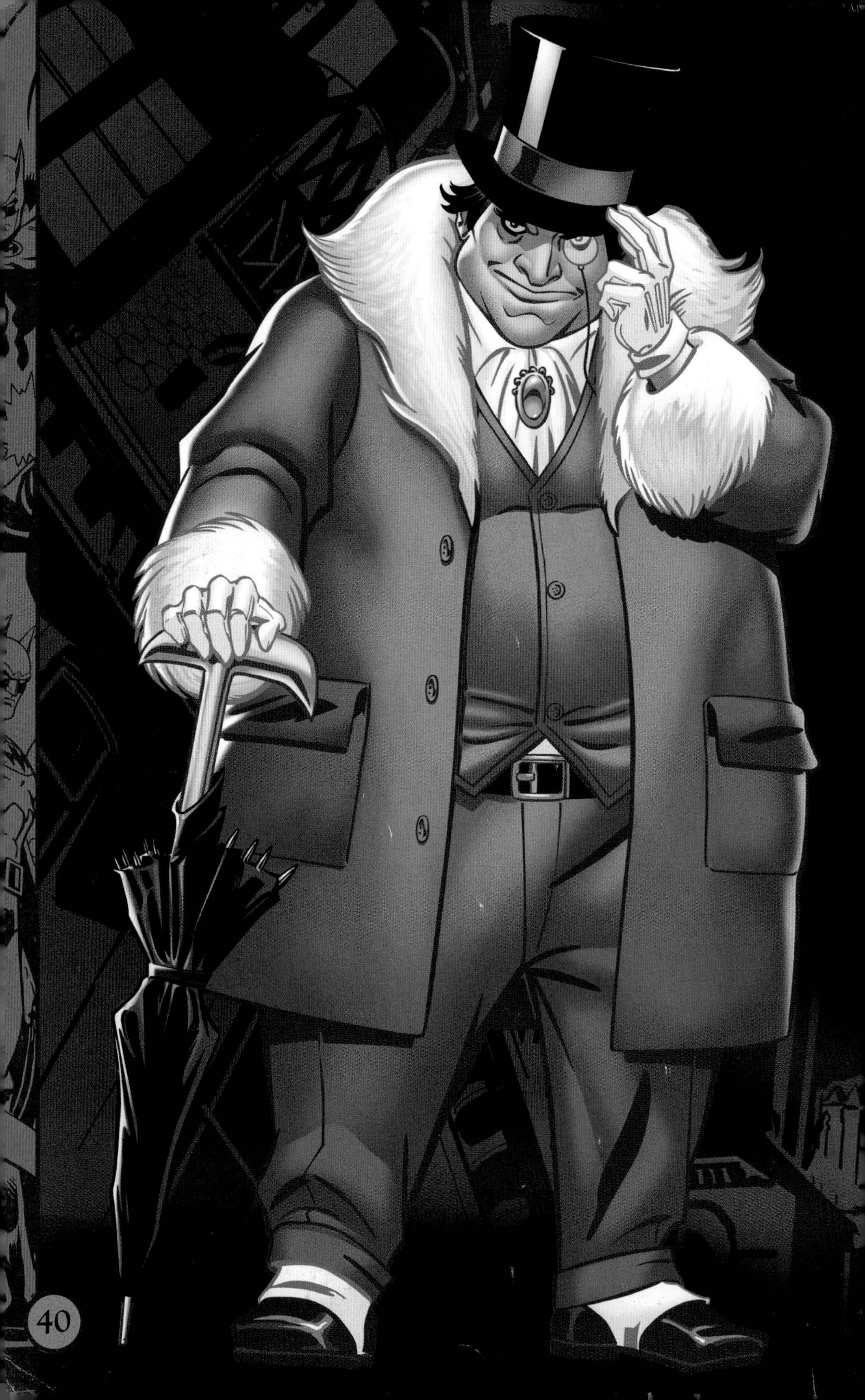

The Penguin

The Penguin is a rich crime boss in Gotham City. He has a special umbrella which he uses as a weapon. The Penguin has tried lots of strange schemes to make money. Once he even tried to train birds to commit crimes for him. But Batman always defeats the Penguin!

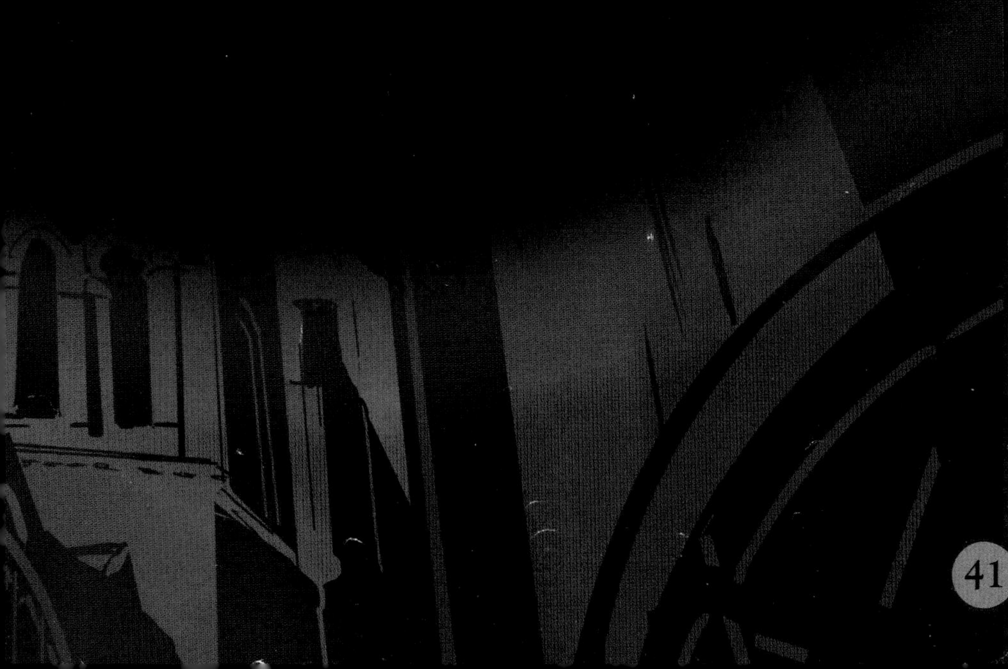

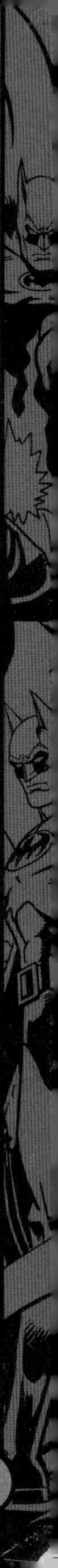

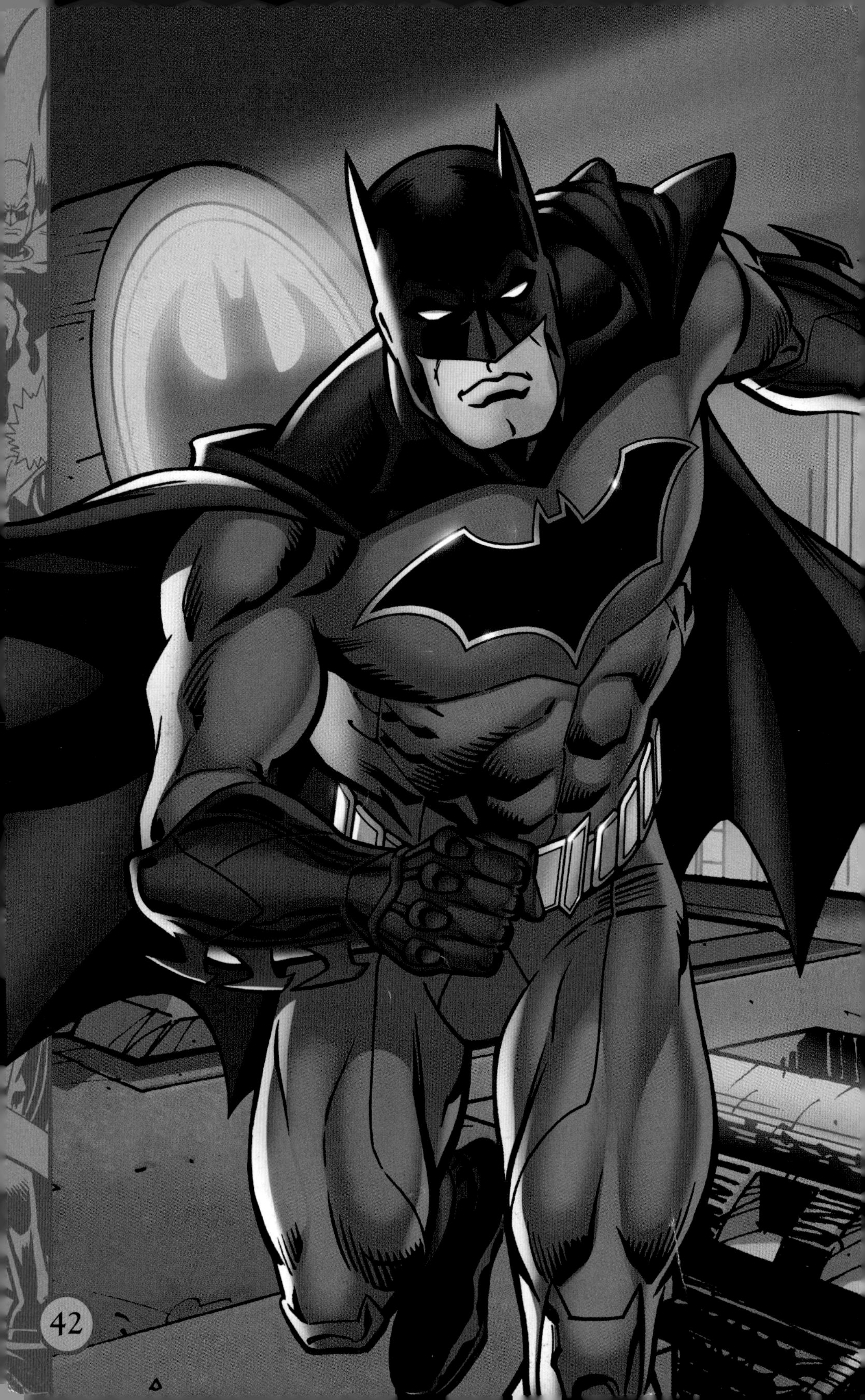

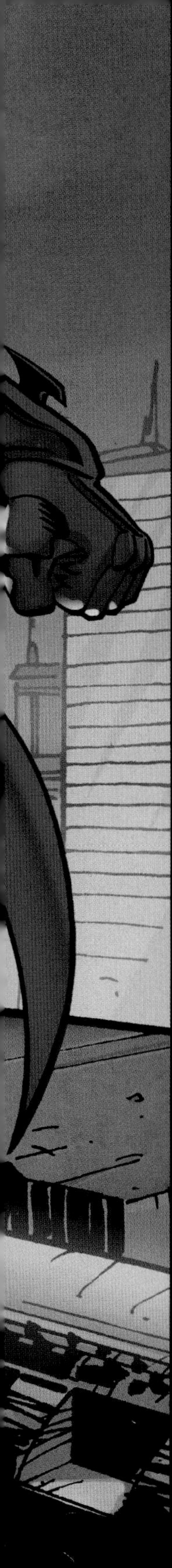

The Dark Knight

Batman is always ready to protect the people of Gotham City. He has had to face dangerous Super-Villains and criminals. But Batman has also inspired many other Super Heroes and allies to help him. When people see The Dark Knight, he gives them hope.

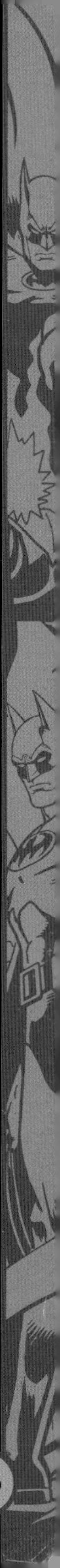

Quiz

1. Who is in charge of the police in Gotham City?

2. What is Batman's secret identity?

3. Where is the Batcave located?

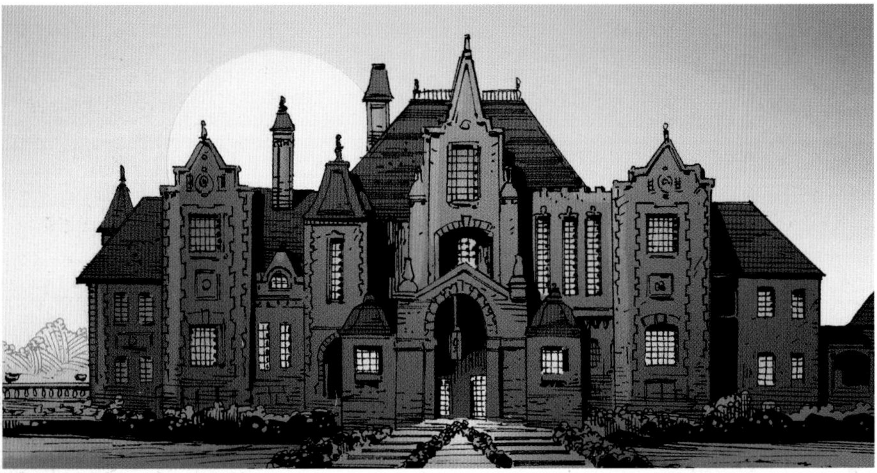

4. What is the name of Batman's car?

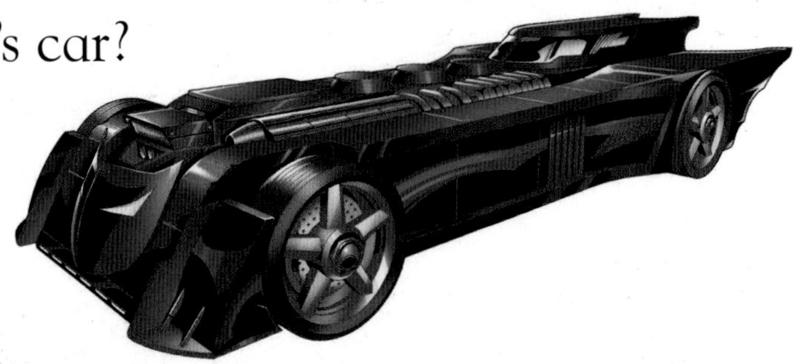

5. Who are the Dynamic Duo?

6. True or false? The Riddler is in the Bat-Family.

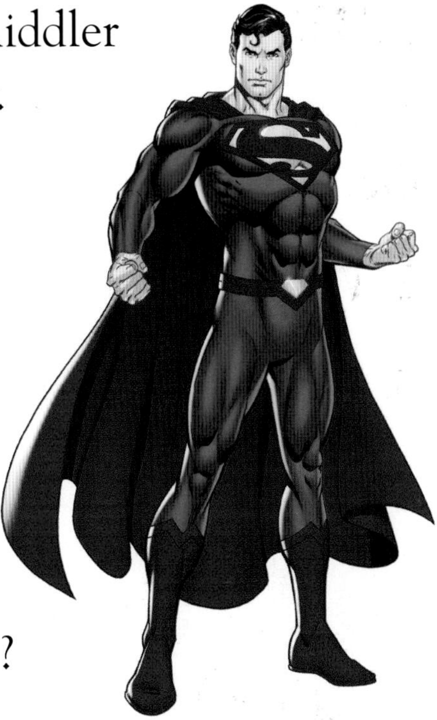

7. Which planet is Superman from?

8. Has The Joker been sent to Arkham Asylum?

9. Where did Harley Quinn used to work?

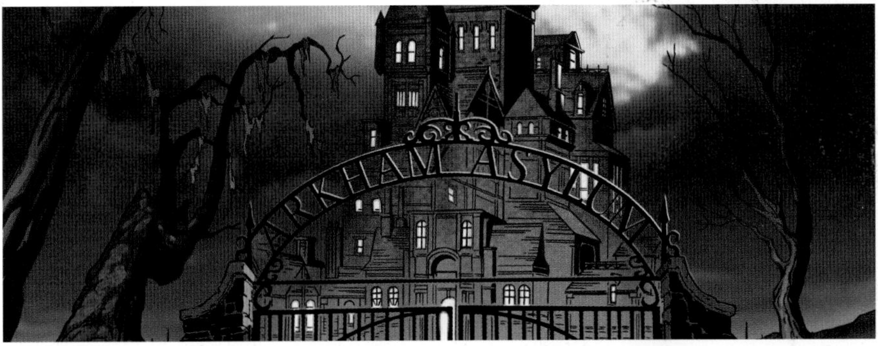
ARKHAM ASYLUM

10. What weapon does the Penguin use?

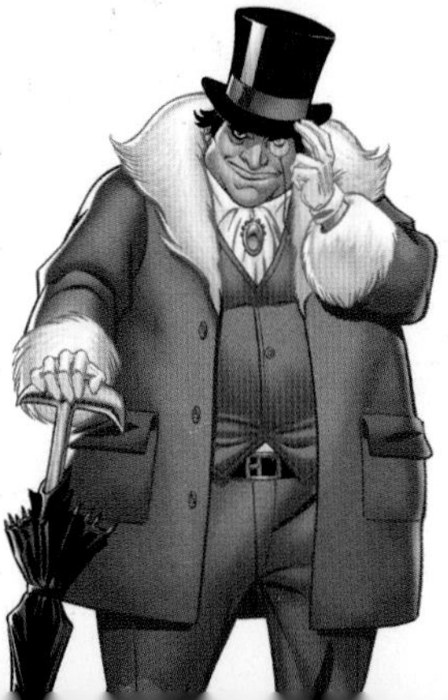

Answers on page 47

Glossary

agile
to move and think quickly and easily.

burglar
someone who breaks into buildings to steal items.

CEO
a person who is the leader of an organization
or business.

cowl
a hood or hooded cloak.

grappling hook
a hook connected to a rope which can attach to
a surface.

identity
who a person is.

robot
a machine that looks and acts like a living creature.

scheme
a crafty or secret plan.

technology
equipment and machines that help people.

Index

Answers to the quiz on pages 44 and 45:

1. Commissioner Gordon 2. Bruce Wayne 3. Under Wayne Manor 4. The Batmobile 5. Batman and Robin 6. False 7. Krypton 8. Yes 9. Arkham Asylum 10. An umbrella

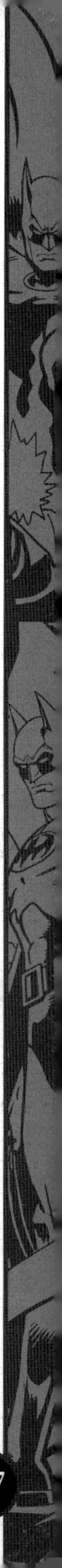

A LEVEL FOR EVERY READER

This book is a part of an exciting four-level reading series to support children in developing the habit of reading widely for both pleasure and information. Each book is designed to develop a child's reading skills, fluency, grammar awareness, and comprehension in order to build confidence and enjoyment when reading.

Ready for a Level 2 (Beginning to Read) book

A child should:

- be able to recognize a bank of common words quickly and be able to blend sounds together to make some words.
- be familiar with using beginner letter sounds and context clues to figure out unfamiliar words.
- sometimes correct his/her reading if it doesn't look right or make sense.
- be aware of the need for a slight pause at commas and a longer one at periods.

A valuable and shared reading experience

For many children, reading requires much effort, but adult participation can make reading both fun and easier. Here are a few tips on how to use this book with a young reader:

Check out the contents together:

- read about the book on the back cover and talk about the contents page to help heighten interest and expectation.
- discuss new or difficult words.
- chat about labels, annotations, and pictures.

Support the reader:

- give the book to the young reader to turn the pages.
- where necessary, encourage longer words to be broken into syllables, sound out each one, and then flow the syllables together; ask him/her to reread the sentence to check the meaning.
- encourage the reader to vary her/his voice as she/he reads; demonstrate how to do this if helpful.

Talk at the end of each book, or after every few pages:

- ask questions about the text and the meaning of the words used—this helps develop comprehension skills.
- read the quiz at the end of the book and encourage the reader to answer the questions, if necessary, by turning back to the relevant pages to find the answers.

Series consultant, Dr. Linda Gambrell, Distinguished Professor of Education at Clemson University, has served as President of the National Reading Conference, the College Reading Association, and the International Reading Association.